"Tell me how we met then?"

Rebecca stopped walking and there."

"Out where?"

"In the ocean. Ten years ago you saved m—
She started walking again. "And when I offered my heart to you, you turned me away."

He blinked and didn't move. No, it couldn't be. "Becca? You're little Becca?"

She threw out her arms and kept walking, increasing the distance between them. "As you can see, I'm not little anymore. And I know it's best to stay away from you. You once called me a little mouse."

"I know," he said, walking up to her, easily catching up to her.

"Yes, but the little mouse now knows better than to play with the lion."

He shoved his hands in his pockets. "I didn't mean to hurt you—"

"What's past is past."

"And I don't see you as a mouse anymore."

She stopped and looked up at him. "I'm glad, because I want you to picture me as something else."

"What?"

"A dragonfly that you will never catch."

He shook his head. "I can't."

"Why not?"

"Because I have every intention of catching you."

Dear Reader,

Tales of my great-great-grandfather, a rebel who grew up on the island of Jamaica, helped to flavor my imagination for the arrogant Aaron Wethers in *Touch of Paradise*. The talented Rebecca Cromwell came to me after I attended a fashion show for a local designer.

This story of sun, sand and seduction led to questions of *"What if…"*

What if a misunderstanding tore apart two people who were clearly meant for each other? What if a pet iguana helped reunite them? What if someone turned paradise into a dangerous puzzle?

What if…

Well, you get the idea. Finding the answers to these questions led to a journey of twists and turns and the ultimate romance.

Enjoy,

Dara Girard

Touch
OF
Paradise

DARA GIRARD

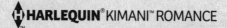
HARLEQUIN® KIMANI™ ROMANCE

Recycling programs
for this product may
not exist in your area.

ISBN-13: 978-0-373-86407-2

Touch of Paradise

Copyright © 2015 by Sade Odubiyi

For questions and comments about the quality of this book please contact us
at CustomerService@Harlequin.com.

Printed in U.S.A.

Dara Girard fell in love with storytelling at an early age. Her romance writing career happened by chance when she discovered the power of a happy ending. She is an award-winning author whose novels are known for their sense of humor, interesting plot twists and witty dialogue. When she's not writing, she enjoys spring mornings and autumn afternoons, French pastries, dancing to the latest hits, and long drives.

Dara loves to hear from her readers. You can reach her at contactdara@daragirard.com or PO Box 10345, Silver Spring, MD 20914.

Books by Dara Girard

Harlequin Kimani Romance

Pages of Passion
Beneath the Covers
All I Want Is You
Secret Paradise
A Reluctant Hero
Perfect Match
Snowed In with the Doctor
Engaging Brooke
Her Tender Touch
Touch of Paradise

Visit the Author Profile page at Harlequin.com for more titles.

To my readers.

Chapter 1

The luscious, exotic island of St. James boasted white sand beaches, towering coconut and breadfruit trees and water so blue it put the sky to shame. Red Beacon Villa Resorts sat on the far north side, away from the island's bustling capital and other major cities. The resort was an international destination that catered to an array of guests and had done so for the past fifty years. Its majestic main house stood proud and welcoming. But while outside a soft Caribbean breeze toyed with the palm trees that surrounded the house's tall pillars and gleaming windows, a storm raged within.

"She said *what*?" Aaron Wethers asked, glaring at the man who faced him. A little green lizard sat outside on the windowsill, seeming to look at the two men who sat in the office. One man sat behind a large oak desk decorated with intricate, inlaid gold trim. He was considerably younger than the second man and nearly twice his size, and his steady gaze seemed to make the second man sink lower in his chair.

The second man was Harvey Clark, a name he'd hated since he was a boy, but he'd never had the courage to change it, so he preferred to go by the initials H.C. Harvey wiped the sweat from his forehead with a handkerchief and fought not to chew his nails. It was a nervous habit he'd finally conquered in his late forties. The room wasn't hot, but under Wethers's stare, he felt like an ant under a microscope. He'd practiced what he was going to say all yesterday and even this morning before the meeting, but nothing could have prepared him for the anger that flashed in his boss's penetrating dark gaze.

Wethers was a man both respected and, at times, feared. He was the kind of man who could make anyone feel small with just a glance. Not due to arrogance, although as a child of privilege it was almost expected, or because he was a bully—he was a fair man and loyal to his staff. Harvey liked him. He'd worked for his father and was honored to work with the son. But the younger Wethers was a man you didn't want to disappoint, and one you certainly didn't want to make angry. Harvey lightened his tone, attempting not to make the news sound as bad as it really was. "Your sister needs your help."

Aaron fell silent, then slowly blinked with the ease of a lazy lion. "What the hell do I know about hosting a fashion show?" he finally asked.

"You don't have to know anything. That's not what she needs you for."

"What, then?"

"She thinks someone is trying to sabotage the show. A box of props went missing."

"And we had a new shipment sent. I know. I had a friend of mine take care of replacing the items. I'd hardly call that sabotage."

Harvey wiped his neck, then glanced outside and saw Wethers's son, Brandon, looking through the bushes. "But your sister is nervous because other things have gone wrong."

"My sister tends to dramatize issues." Wethers kept his gaze focused on the magnificent view of the ocean from his office window.

"Right now she's in the process of leaving the island with three of her models who've developed rashes all over their bodies."

"An allergic reaction?"

"She thinks someone tampered with their makeup. She's taking several samples with her to get tested."

"She could have had someone else do that."

"Your mother said—"

Wethers lifted his brows. "You're actually going to bring my mother into this, too?"

Harvey silently swore, knowing he'd made a wrong move. Hitting Wethers with both his mother and sister was not a wise strategy. "She agrees with your sister. They both think your involvement is essential."

Aaron rubbed his chin. "And you're just telling me this now? My sister couldn't tell me this yesterday?"

"The makeup tampering—"

Aaron held up his hand. "Alleged tampering."

"—really concerns her. She wouldn't have bothered you otherwise," Harvey finished, then glanced outside again, unable to hold Wethers's steady gaze, and saw Brandon talking to one of the groundskeepers, who listened to something he said, then shook his head. What was the boy looking for?

"H.C.?"

Harvey turned sharply to him. "Yes?"

"What are you looking at?"

"Your son."

Wethers's tone sharpened. "What about my son?"

Harvey shook his head, sorry he'd mentioned it. Wethers had enough to think about, and Harvey didn't want to worry him needlessly. It was probably nothing. Brandon was a good kid and didn't usually get into trouble. "Nothing. Sorry, I—I just saw him run past." He folded his damp handkerchief and pressed it to his forehead again.

Wethers narrowed his eyes. "What's got you so nervous?"

Harvey shrugged. "I'm not nervous." He adjusted his position in the large overstuffed chair.

Wethers narrowed his eyes a fraction more. "You believe her, don't you?"

"These incidents don't seem like accidents, especially the last one."

Aaron shrugged. "Two mishaps aren't—"

"Three."

"Excuse me?"

"Actually, there have been three mishaps. These two were just the latest. The first one involved the digital file for the event. It somehow got corrupted, but fortunately there was a backup."

"Hmm."

"She really sounded upset on the phone about what's happening."

Aaron groaned. "I hate this. You know my plan was to stay as far away as possible over these next several days while our resort is overrun with over-indulged, self-interested parasites."

Harvey held out his hands. "I know you had a bad experience with models—"

"Bad? Would you call the sinking of the *Titanic* merely bad? The stock market crash of 1929 a mere miscalculation?"

Harvey sighed. "I'm sorry. I know how bad…I mean awful—" he quickly corrected "—it was for you. But that was more than nine years ago. This isn't about vanity. I've seen some of what they're putting together and it's really beautiful, and the people I've met have been very nice. We're dealing with professionals, and I'll help as much as I can, but I think your sister's concern shouldn't be taken lightly."

Aaron slowly stood to his feet. "You're a good man, H.C." Aaron walked around the desk, then leaned against it with his arms folded. "I love my sister, but she has a habit of causing trouble, and my mother indulges her. But maybe there is something to this. When is my mother coming?"

Harvey nervously cleared his throat, wishing Wethers would return to his seat. He hated having to look up at him. "Your—your mother?"

"Yes, my mother. This is right up her alley. If she's as concerned as my sister, she'll love to be here and make sure everything is spectacular. She's been a fashion hound since I was a kid. She'll use this opportunity to indulge her personal hobby. I don't care if she wants to come and boss me around a bit while I look into what's going on."

Harvey unfolded his damp handkerchief and wiped his forehead, his cheeks and his neck, then crumpled it in his fist. This was the news he didn't want to deliver. "That's the problem."

Aaron stilled. "What is?"

"Your mother needs you to be in charge."

"Me? Why?"

"She broke her ankle while vacationing in Switzerland and won't be able to be here, either."

Wethers looked out the window at the swaying palm trees and said in a low voice, "How convenient."

"It doesn't sound very convenient to me."

Wethers shifted his gaze back to Harvey. "You missed the ring of sarcasm. I'll try to be clearer next time." He tapped a finger against his lips and said in a quiet voice, "I wonder what those two are up to?"

"I really think your sister's frightened."

"Then why didn't she tell me directly?"

"She didn't think you'd believe her. And this event is very important to her. This new designer is making waves around the globe. Red Beacon Villa Resorts will make a name for itself hosting the Cromwell Collection."

"I don't care what his name is—"

"Her. Her name is Rebecca Cromwell," Harvey continued, ignoring Aaron's obvious boredom with the topic.

Aaron stared at him for a long moment, making it clear he didn't care.

Harvey swallowed. He hated when Wethers pinned

him with that penetrating look. "I just thought you should know."

"Tell me."

"Tell you what?"

"What you really think. Should I be concerned?"

"I honestly don't know," Harvey said, relieved that at least that was the truth. "There are a lot of people involved in this event—volunteers, caterers, photographers, the stage crew, the stylists. Mistakes are bound to happen."

"You're giving me excuses, not an opinion. What do you really think?"

"I think that if what Candace believes is true, we have a serious problem because things seem to be escalating. The corrupted file and lost props were an annoyance, but tampering with the model's makeup makes things more dangerous. Only the top three models were affected, and they were to be the key draw for the event, since one of them is a local girl. If anything else goes wrong, it's possible we'll have to cancel."

"I'm not going to let that happen. We may have lost three days, but we have eleven days left."

"Yes, sir," Harvey said, feeling his heart cheer. He knew Wethers would do whatever it took to save the show.

"I want to meet with security in an hour."

"Yes." Harvey nodded, then left the room, wiping his forehead again when his phone rang. "Hello?"

"What does he think?" Candace Wethers said.

Harvey lowered his voice. "You should have told him yourself."

"You know I couldn't. Was he angry?"

"Yes, at first, then he said he'll look into it."

"Did you tell him about Rebecca?"

"Only briefly. I thought it best to focus on the show. I don't think he'll believe she's the one being targeted. Besides, there's no proof."

"I know, but I just have a bad feeling about this. I think whoever is trying to sabotage the show is trying to hurt her."

"You think her life's in danger?"

Candace sighed. "I really don't know. It doesn't make sense, but I have a horrible feeling that Rebecca could get hurt in more ways than one."

"Do you think perhaps we should reschedule or cancel the show?"

"No," she said quickly. "Don't even think that. I know that Aaron can do this."

"Are you sure you know what you're doing?"

Candace laughed in a way that made Harvey nervous. "I always know what I'm doing."

Aaron studied the lizard sunning on his windowsill. "If it were just Candace and my mother I wouldn't care much, but it's not like H.C. to worry," he said, talking to the creature. "I can't have that, but Candace knew I wanted to stay out of this fashion thing." Was she faking this crazy story about sabotage? No, it would be too easy to verify. And she wouldn't leave a key event, like a high-profile fashion show, just to annoy him. Although he wouldn't put much past her. She liked to get her way and thought his life was dull. Was this her way of adding some spice?

The lizard looked at him briefly, then darted away. Aaron rested his hands on the window frame and looked out at the ocean. Was it wrong to want a quiet, simple life? His sister always wanted more. More friends, more excitement, more fun. That's why she trotted across the globe while he stayed on St. James, raising his son. She was the creative one in the family. She was the one who loved fashion and art. She was beautiful, reckless, changeable and irresistible. He'd idolized her so much as a child that, as a grown man, he'd married a woman similar to her, and that had been a disaster.

His marriage to Ina Margarita Sheldon had shown him just how much he and his sister were dissimilar. He was practical and rational and would never change, although his sister continued to try to encourage him to do so. He remembered their conversation last month as they sat on the veranda of the main house, where he and his son lived. His mother and sister each had their own separate small three-bedroom chalet, located several hundred feet away from his residence, but Candace always liked to stop by to chat, scold or tease him, depending on her mood.

"You can do better," she said, nibbling on a fresh slice of melon. A large pink pinwheel hat shaded her face.

"What are you talking about?" Aaron asked as he watched his sister make her way through the plate full of fruit.

"Mary, the new woman you're seeing."

Aaron shook his head and speared a mango cube. "Her name is Martha Banyan."

"And she's a librarian."

"She's a teacher." He pointed his fork at her. "I knew I shouldn't have said anything."

"I'm glad you did. I would have found out anyway. You know news travels fast on this island. I just know you can do better."

Aaron set his fork down, no longer interested in eating. "I thought you'd be impressed."

"Impressed by what? Plain, boring, dull—"

"She's pretty and sweet."

"I wasn't talking about how she looks. I was talking about her clothes."

"Not all women are interested in fashion like you, or can afford to change their wardrobe every season."

Candace made a face. "There's no need to exaggerate."

Aaron grinned. "I thought I was being conservative."

Candace rolled her eyes and swung her foot. "She's just not the right one for you."

Aaron sat back and folded his arms, trying to keep his tone neutral, although his sister's criticism bothered him. "I thought you'd at least be happy for me. You're the one who's been pressuring me to start dating again."

"Settling for the first woman who said yes was not what I meant."

Aaron frowned. "I'm not settling."

"She's everything Ina isn't."

"Exactly." He speared a large slice of pineapple with his fork.

"You shouldn't sound so proud of it." Candace waved her fork at him before she stabbed another melon slice. "You're going to bored with her. You're a lot wilder than you think, little brother. Remember, you've got the blood of a pirate running through you."

"I'm nothing like our ancestor," Aaron said, picking up his fork again, feeling suddenly restless. He hated the comparison. It made him seem more mysterious than he actually was. "That's what disappointed Ina the most. She thought she was marrying someone else." Early in their marriage, he discovered she had bought into their ancestral history and thought she had married a "rogue," and was very disappointed.

"She was stupid. She didn't know what she had."

"Martha is good with Brandon."

"Of course she is," Candace said, waving her hand in a dismissive gesture. "She's a librarian, for goodness' sake."

"Teacher," Aaron corrected.

"See?" Candace waved her hand again, as if he'd just proven her point. "She's paid to be good with children."

"And she's smart and—"

Candace shook her head again. "And she's still wrong for you."

"She loves this island as much as I do, she likes my son and she likes me."

Candace set her fork down. "Are you thinking of marrying her?"

"It's too soon for that, but—"

"But you're thinking about it?" She removed her sunglasses and stared directly at him.

"I'm ready to marry again," he said, avoiding her gaze.

Candace sighed and folded her arms. "Promise me one thing."

He looked at her. "What?"

"Don't get too serious about her until after the fashion show."

A month later, Candace's words still echoed in his head. Aaron turned from the window, trying to let the memory of that talk fade, but it wouldn't leave him. He still found the request odd. He was a grown man. He didn't need his older sister's blessing on anything. But he still remembered the look on her face when she asked him to wait until *after* the show. He recalled how sly she looked. But if she thought surrounding him with an endless supply of beautiful women would change his mind, she'd be disappointed. But would she go this far to get him involved? He sighed when he heard a quiet knock on the door.

"Come in," he said, returning to his desk.

His eight-year-old son, Brandon, entered and he felt some of his annoyance subside. His son was the only thing he didn't regret about his marriage. "What is it?" he asked with a smile.

Brandon bit his lip. "Promise you won't get mad."

"I can't promise you that, but tell me anyway."

"I've looked everywhere."

Aaron's smile fell. "Looked for what?"

"Can you please promise not to get mad?" Brandon said, nervously playing with his fingers and turning his feet inward.

He stood. "Brandon."

"At least don't shout," he said, straightening his shoulders and trying to look brave.

Aaron folded his arms. "What happened?"

Brandon hung his head and spoke to the floor. "Trident is missing."

Chapter 2

As a child, Rebecca Cromwell feared the monster under the bed. At twenty-nine, she finally saw it. It was the last straw. Her nerves were already frayed due to three days where everything had gone wrong. Since landing on St. James, she'd faced one mishap after another and feared that the latest incident would severely hamper the success of her upcoming fashion show.

She'd hoped for some time to decompress, since over the past three days she'd hardly slept or eaten. After scrambling to find replacements for the three models she'd lost, she'd decided to take a long, hot shower and enjoy one of the luxurious amenities in her spacious suite. It was one of thirty private villas that lined the secluded cove where Red Beacon Villa Resorts was located. She could see the sun's rays dancing along the crystal clear waters from one of her many palatial windows.

Humming to herself, she'd left her bathroom and crossed the cool bare marble floors, and she'd planned on a quick nap when she saw a green head with dark eyes peek out from the shadowy depths under her bed. She screamed and jumped on the mattress. That's when she thought that being on *top* of the monster was worse than seeing the monster, so she jumped off the bed and up on a chair.

"Rebecca!" Her assistant, Kelli Davis, pounded on her front door. "Are you okay?"

"It's open."

Kelli rushed into the room with her hair uncombed, half-dressed, her shirt still hanging off her shoulder and jeans unzipped. She stared up at her. "What's wrong?"

Rebecca pointed with a shaky finger. "There's something under my bed."

Kelli grinned. "Giant dust bunnies?"

"No, something big and green. Don't look!" she said when Kelli bent down to look under the bed.

"Then how am I supposed to see what it is?"

"I already told you what it is."

Kelli ignored her and lifted the sheet, then screamed, stumbling back. "Oh, my God, you're right. It's huge. We have to kill it." She madly looked around for something to grab, just in case the thing came out from under the bed and tried to attack her, but couldn't find anything.

"I'm not going to kill it."

"Then what are you going to do?" Kelli finished zipping up her pants and adjusted her top.

"Get someone to get rid of it." Rebecca jumped

down from the chair and ran out the front door, and smack into a wall. Or what she'd at first thought was a wall before something grabbed her and kept her from falling backward. She gingerly touched her face, her nose still stinging from the impact, then glanced up and nearly screamed again.

It was him. Mr. Beautiful. Mr. Wonderful. The man who'd once been the object of her dreams. Her hero— Aaron Wethers. The man who'd broken her heart ten years ago.

Just like everything else in his life, time seemed to have given him an advantage, broadening his shoulders, refining his impressive physique. The wind and the sun seemed to have ripened the beauty of his brown skin, making his handsome features almost majestic. And her traitorous heart responded to his compelling, golden-brown gaze.

She knew she'd see him again, but she hadn't planned on a moment like this. She had planned on returning to St. James as a success, so that he could see how much she'd changed. She'd planned to be cool and suave, and hoped to seduce him by showing off her gorgeous figure, casting a glance in his direction then ignoring him. But now her show was in trouble and she'd crashed into him after racing out of her villa with no makeup on, her hair in total disarray and wearing just her bathrobe.

"Are you okay?" he asked.

Goodness, even his voice was better than she remembered. Deep and intoxicating as rum punch, his island lilt made her want to step closer and listen more. "I'm fine," Rebecca said in a voice that was too high. She gathered her robe close around her and tightened the sash, wishing she'd at least put on her bra and panties, but she hadn't, and at that moment she felt vulnerable and bare. "Perfectly fine," she said with a wave of her hand. She tried to brush her hair into place, but it wouldn't cooperate.

"Fine?" Kelli squealed behind her. "There's a giant—"

"It's nothing," Rebecca said with a light laugh, seeing that all the commotion was attracting an audience. It was then that she saw a miniature version of Aaron looking anxious beside him. The little boy looked up at Aaron, then her, then his gaze dropped to the ground. Rebecca immediately guessed the situation. Her monster was likely his pet. And it had escaped. Rebecca knew how they responded could really hurt Aaron's image if other guests knew what she and Kelli had found.

Rebecca bent down to the little boy's level and said in a low voice, "You look worried, but you don't have to be. It's okay."

He lifted his gaze to hers, his big brown eyes hopeful. "You found Trident?"

"I think so," Rebecca whispered, aware that people were watching them closely. "But you'll have to check."

Aaron shook his head. "I'm really so—"

Rebecca straightened and screamed again, this time like a woman arriving at an airport and seeing a long-lost friend. "It's so good to see you again," she said, hugging the little boy, even though he looked at her, startled. "You've grown so tall!" She turned to Aaron and screamed like a fashionista seeing an outfit she adored, then hugged him, too. "It's been ages, darling. Kiss, kiss." She kissed his cheeks, then waved them inside. "Come in, come in." She glanced at an older couple who watched them with a frown. She winked at them, then turned. Once they were all inside, she closed the door and pointed to the bed. "Trident is under there."

The little boy looked up at her, curious. "Why did you scream and hug us like that?"

"Because I didn't want people asking questions."

He giggled. "You acted really silly. Like one of Aunt Candace's friends."

Aaron nudged him. "You shouldn't be laughing. What should you be saying?"

"Oh, yes. I'm sorry, miss."

Rebecca nodded. "You're forgiven."

"Now go get Trident," Aaron said.

The little boy rushed forward and lifted the sheets. "Trident, you're in big trouble."

"I'm very sorry about this," Aaron said.

"What is it?" Rebecca asked, once the boy had coaxed the creature from under the bed.

"A giant iguana. He must have snuck in when they were cleaning your villa. The maids keep the door open to air the room," Aaron said with a note of apology.

"I understand how he got in, but how are you going to get him out of here without anyone noticing? I assume you don't want anyone to know that Trident escaped."

Aaron ran a tired hand down his face, then looked around as if considering his options. "You're right."

He looked at the little boy. "Didn't I tell you to keep an eye on him?"

"I'm really sorry, Dad."

Even though she'd guessed that the little boy was his, hearing him call Aaron Dad validated her assumption. Strangely, fatherhood looked good on him. Rebecca mentally shook her head. She didn't care. She'd come to St. James to show him what a success she had become and what he'd lost. She would remain calm, collected and distant. "I have an idea, but you have to wait. First, I have to change." Rebecca excused herself, grabbed some clothes from her closet, then disappeared into the bathroom.

"Get a hold of yourself," Rebecca mumbled to herself as she quickly changed. "It doesn't matter that he's still gorgeous or that he has a cute little boy. He doesn't even remember you. The jerk." She stared at her reflection. "You are going to help him this one time, and then you're going to ignore him. You didn't come here to fall for him all over again. Your career and this fashion show are all that matter." She pointed at her image. "Are we clear?" She quickly massaged ointment in her hair and put on some lip gloss, then left the bathroom, ready to deal with the issue at hand.

She told Aaron her idea. At first he was skeptical, but then he agreed. He called the maid service and requested they bring a large laundry trolley to the villa. When it arrived, Aaron set Trident inside, then Rebecca and the maid covered the iguana with several sheets and towels. "Now nobody will ever know I had a surprise visitor," Rebecca said, pleased.

Aaron looked at the maid. "You know what to do. Make it quick. He can't be under there too long."

She nodded. "Yes, sir."

The little boy took Rebecca's hand. "Come on."

Aaron grabbed his son's shoulder. "What are you doing?"

Brandon looked up at his father, affronted. "I'm going to show her where Trident lives."

"You have to ask permission first."

"Oh, right," he said, looking contrite. "Dad, can I take her to show—"

"No, you have to ask *her* permission."

The little boy turned to Rebecca. "Can I show you where Trident lives?"

"I'm sorry," Rebecca said. "But I have a lot to do today. Perhaps another time."

The little boy looked disappointed but nodded. "Okay. I'll come back later."

"No," Aaron said. "You'll call and make sure she's free."

"But, Dad—"

"We'll talk about this later. Go."

The little boy sighed, started to leave, then turned. "I didn't tell you my name. I'm Brandon Wethers," he said, holding out his hand.

"I'm Rebecca Cromwell."

"Do you have any kids?"

"No."

"Are you married?"

Aaron nudged him toward the door. "That's enough."

"My dad's not married."

Aaron shoved him a little harder. "Get out of here."

"I'm just trying to help. Aunt Candace says women always want to know that about you."

Aaron held up his hand. "One more word, and I will get angry."

Brandon nodded, then waved. "Bye, Miss Rebecca."

Rebecca grinned. "Bye."

Brandon looked at her for a long moment, then tugged on his father's shirt. Aaron bent down, and the boy whispered something in his ear.

"No," Aaron said.

Brandon gripped his hands together. "Please."

"Go home."

Brandon made a face, then left.

"Your son is a character," Kelli said, walking up to Aaron. "But he had the right idea. You've already met Rebecca, but let me introduce myself. I'm Kelli Davis." She held out her hand like a canary offering herself to a cat. The red highlights in her black hair caught the light, and she lowered and raised her eyes in a way that made her interest clear. She had taken the time, during all the commotion, to make sure she looked presentable.

He shook her hand. "Aaron Wethers."

She grinned. "It's nice to know we have something in common."

"And what's that?"

She winked. "I'm not married, either."

Aaron nodded, making no indication what he thought of her statement, and turned to Rebecca. "There's no excuse for what just happened. Let me offer you a complimentary dinner and spa treatment at the VIP lounge."

"That's really not necessary," Rebecca said, embarrassed by her assistant's flirtation.

"Yes, it is. I was just made aware of the other troubles you've had since you arrived, and this incident with my son's pet iguana is unacceptable. I'm looking into what's going on." He pulled out his wallet and gave her a card. "Just give them this."

"You really don't—"

His cell phone rang, interrupting her. "I have to take this. Excuse me," he said, then walked outside.

Rebecca nodded and watched him leave.

Kelli snatched the card from her and studied it. "You lucky girl. A free dinner and spa."

"You can have it."

Kelli stared at her, surprised. "Why?"

He didn't remember her. She'd hoped her name would have meant something, but saying it hadn't triggered a memory. Not even a little. Of course, it had been ten years, but when they had met, it had been such a monumental moment in her life. She had hoped she'd made some impact on him. What was the point of trying to ignore him or show him how successful she'd become when he didn't even know who she was? "I'll be too busy to use it," Rebecca said.

Kelli eagerly tucked the card away, as if she were afraid Rebecca would change her mind. "Well, if you're sure."

"I'm positive," Rebecca said, then reached out and pinched her.

"Ow!" Kelli said, rubbing her arm. "What did you do that for?"

"Because you know I hate when you flirt in front of me. I don't care what you do on your own time, but when you're with me I expect you to be a professional."

"I'm sorry, I couldn't help myself. I mean, don't you think—"

"It doesn't matter what I think. His family owns this resort and—"

Kelli started to fan herself. "Oh, yes, he's Candace's brother. Just my type."

Yes, Candace's brother. Candace had tried to bring up the subject of her brother with Rebecca numerous times, since the first day they'd arrived, but she'd always found a way to avoid the topic, preferring to pretend that she'd decided to host her collection at their resort because it was convenient rather than because of their shared past. And with the recent mishaps, it hadn't been hard for her to focus on something other than him. Now Candace was gone, and Aaron had taken her place. Rebecca couldn't afford to have anything else go wrong. Worst of all, she didn't want him to see her as the helpless damsel she'd been all those years ago.

"Find someone else."

Kelli raised a brow. "Are you interested?"

"No. I just don't want you distracted. We're here on business."

"I'll be discreet, then."

"Good."

Kelli folded her arms, sending Rebecca a significant look. "Are you sure you're not interested?"

"I don't have time to be interested in anyone."

"It's been two years since your breakup. Don't you think—"

"I think you have too much time on your hands. I want to take a nap before I meet with the stage director."

Kelli sighed and left. But Rebecca didn't take a nap. She couldn't sleep. Kelli was on the prowl, and Rebecca couldn't blame her. Aaron was a worthy target. She'd been just as eager to get his attention ten years ago, but for a different reason…

Ten years ago

It was really hard to run in three-inch high heels. Even harder to run on a boat, away from a drunken college sophomore she had only just met that evening, who wanted to bed as many coeds as he could on spring break. "Come on, don't be like that," he said. Although his words were slurred, his pace was incredibly steady.

"I said leave me alone!" Rebecca shouted over her shoulder. She could see the lights of the island in the distance. The sun had set an hour ago, but there was still a purple haze that colored the sky. She knew she couldn't make a swim for it. She wished she hadn't decided to go on the two-level rental party boat and had stayed in her room with her roommate, Marie, instead.

"I just think we'll have a good time together," she had told Marie.

She'd heard the rumors and knew what some of the boys expected. Her two other friends were already giving his buddies "good times" somewhere on the boat, but this wasn't the kind of holiday she'd been hoping for. She'd wanted to go sailing, laze on the beach, shop in one of the crowded outdoor markets. Instead, she'd found herself getting crushed at a keg party, and now running from a drunken college guy who had arms like an octopus. One of those arms reached her and pulled her to him.

"You know, your little act is getting old."

Rebecca tried to shove him away. He smelled of stale aftershave and beer. "It's not an act. I'm not interested."

He looked her over. "It's not like you should be picky. There are prettier girls out here."

"Then find one of them." She tried hard to push him off her, but he held her even closer.

"Why? I've got you right here." He leaned in to kiss her.

She bit his lip.

He swore and shoved her back, calling her a foul name. "You think that was funny?" he said, touching his lip and seeing blood on his fingers.

"I warned you." But the look in his eyes let her know that her warning had only enraged him. She started running again, getting enough distance to turn a corner out of sight, but she knew there was no cabin room for her to hide in. So she grabbed the rail and swung herself over the side of the boat, hoping that he would pass her without looking down. She heard his footsteps. Heard him swear and then disappear below deck. She held on a little longer, but soon felt her grip slipping. She started to lift herself back up, glad for the cardio class she'd started to take on campus. She had nearly pulled herself all the way up when the chaser popped up and said, "Gotcha!"

His sudden presence startled her. She lost her grip and started to fall backward. He reached out to grab her, but his attempt was clumsy and had too much force. He managed to grip her sleeve and pulled her forward instead of up, and she hit her head before the soft material of her dress ripped in his fingers and she fell into the water, unconscious.

Chapter 3

Rebecca woke up to the sound of voices. When she opened her eyes, she found she was on a rescue craft, and a young man, dripping wet, leaned over her. "You're going to be okay. No, don't sit up," he said gently, pulling her jacket closer together. Then she remembered she hadn't been wearing a jacket—especially not a man's dinner jacket. She looked up at him and saw his white shirt plastered to his muscled chest. She couldn't really place him. He looked much older than the college crowd. "What happened?"

"I saw you go overboard," he said in a rich island lilt.

"And you saved me?" she said with awe. "I could have been attacked by a shark, or stung by jellyfish or drowned."

The corner of his mouth kicked up in a quick grin. "I did what anyone would have done. But you have to be more careful. How much have you had to drink?"

"Nothing."

"Then what were you doing hanging over the side of the boat?"

"I was trying to get away—" She stiffened and sat up too fast. She held her head as the world started to spin.

He reached out to steady her. "I told you to keep still."

"But where is he? I made him so angry."

The man gently pushed her back down. "Relax. You don't have to worry about him anymore."

"He wouldn't leave me alone."

"He will now," he said in a grim tone. "And the next time someone bothers you, you just come to me…" He lifted his brow in a question.

"Becca," she said.

He nodded. "You have nothing to worry about. You're safe now."

"Who are you?"

"Aaron."

She wanted to ask him more questions, but the boat landed on the island before she could. The EMTs rushed to meet them. Her rescuer spoke to one of the police officers on the scene while one of the EMTs assessed her, taking her vital signs and applying some ointment to the bruise on her forehead. He tried to encourage her to go to the hospital, but she declined. "I just want to go home and go to sleep."

"You've suffered a mild concussion, and going home and sleeping wouldn't be a good idea," he said. "Do you have someone who can be with you through the night?"

"No, but—"

"Then it's best that you come with us." The EMTs began to lead her to the waiting ambulance.

"Please, please," she said, starting to panic. "I really don't want to."

"What's going on here?" Aaron asked, joining them.

The EMT told him the situation. Aaron looked at her. "And you really don't want to go to the hospital? They'll treat you well."

"No," she said. "The last time I saw my mother was in a hospital, and it's a painful place for me."

"Okay. I'll look after her," he said when the EMT started to protest. He waved her forward. "Come on," he said, then started walking.

"I'll really be okay by myself," Rebecca said. "Besides, I have a roommate. She can watch me." Rebecca wasn't sure if Marie would still be in their hotel room, or if she would be out partying in town. But she wasn't going to share that bit of knowledge with him.

He extended his hand and took hers in his. "I'm not going to take that risk. And you don't have to worry—you won't be alone with me. People know me on this island."

That certainly wasn't a worry for her. She could tell by the way the EMTs reacted to him that he was a man people respected. She wondered how long he'd lived on the island and why he'd been on the rental boat. Or was he a foreign vacationer like her? He was the complete opposite of the man who'd been chasing her. But no, *man* was the wrong word. The college drunk had been a boy. Aaron definitely was a man. A gentleman, and that was rare nowadays. He treated her with kindness and made her feel safe. She couldn't stop looking at him. He was like a designer coat marked down to half price—completely irresistible.

"Sorry, I wasn't expecting company," he said as he walked over to a motorcycle that leaned up against a stone fence and lifted the one helmet he had. "Maybe I should call a taxi for you."

"No, I'll be okay."

He handed her the helmet and helped her close the latch before sitting on the bike. When she didn't move, he looked at her, concerned. "What's the matter?"

"I've never ridden one of these before."

Aaron's face split into a wide grin. "I'm not expecting you to drive it." He patted the bike with affection. "She hugs the road and purrs like a kitten. I've never had a problem with her. You'll be safe with me." He raised a brow. "You sure you don't want me to call a taxi?"

Rebecca closed her hands into fists. She had no reason to be nervous, but suddenly she was. Not because of the bike, but because of the man. On the boat and talking to the EMT, he'd look civilized, but on the bike, with his rakish grin, he had a devilish air. But he'd saved her life, and people knew him. Maybe her imagination was just running wild because of the darkening sky and the warm Caribbean breeze. She took a deep breath, then got on and sat behind him.

"You have to hold on," he said.

"What?"

He grabbed her arms and wrapped them around his waist. "I want you to hold on tight. I can't have you falling off the bike now, can I? Ready?"

She could feel the heat of his skin through his wet

shirt, and the muscles of his back pressed to her chest. "Yes."

He revved up the machine, then drove through some of the island's back roads. She'd never seen some of those places before. Too soon he stopped the motorcycle and shut off the engine.

"We're here already?" she said, disappointed.

Aaron laughed. "I thought you'd be glad."

"I was just starting to have fun." She took off the helmet.

"Maybe I'll treat you to a longer ride next time," he said, taking the helmet from her and setting it aside.

Rebecca knew he was saying that just to be nice, but she truly hoped he would. She was about to say so when she looked up and finally saw where they were. A large mansion loomed before her—a mansion with a dark history. "I thought you were taking me back to the hotel." She raced up to Aaron and grabbed his arm. "Wait, where are you going?"

"I'm going inside."

"You can't go inside," she said in a low hiss.

He looked down at her, confused. "Why not?"

"I read about this place," she said, casting an uneasy glance at the large structure. "No one on the island comes to this place. It's owned by this wealthy family who are said to be descendants of the famous pirate Pierre LaCroix."

Rebecca went on to tell the story she had heard about how in the early 1600s, a free black man from France, Pierre LaCroix, traveled to St. James. He immediately fell in love with both the people and the land. That was before Spain discovered and decided to claim the island as part of its sovereignty. Pierre

LaCroix fought along with the people, but when faced with defeat, he escaped and became a pirate instead. He was never captured by the Spanish, who were eventually overrun by the British. "This house belongs to his descendants, who got rich from the gold and jewelry Pierre plundered from Spanish and British ships he and his fellow pirates attacked."

He rested his hands on his hips, amused. "Really?"

"It's even been said that the ghost of LaCroix chooses the bride for the eldest male of the family, and if he doesn't marry the woman selected, he falls to ruin."

Aaron's expression changed, and his voice deepened. "If you're really frightened, it's not too late to go to the hospital."

"Why would I do that? I'm not frightened of you, just of this place."

Aaron blinked and didn't move. It took her a moment to realize that the pose reminded her of something. Or rather, someone. In her search to find information about the island, she'd seen a picture of the pirate Pierre LaCroix, and Aaron now looked eerily like him. Like a man who could laugh at a hundred-foot ocean wave, handle a knife with ease and seduce a woman with just a look. Her heart dropped to her feet. "Oh, no. You're one of them, aren't you?"

He nodded.

"I thought you were here on holiday like me," she said, quickly trying to cover her mistake. But she couldn't tell whether she'd made him annoyed or angry. His face held a blank expression, but his golden-brown gaze hadn't lost its intensity. "What were you doing on the boat?" she asked.

"One of the chaperones fell ill and I stepped in."

"I see. I'm so sorry. I didn't mean—"

He shrugged. "It's okay. I'm used to it." He jerked his thumb to the door. "Are you ready to go in now, or do you want to tell me some more ghost stories?"

Rebecca covered her face, embarrassed. "I've had a traumatic experience. I cannot be accountable for anything I say."

He laughed and took her hand. "Come on."

A maid greeted them the moment they entered. "Please take her to the TV room," Aaron said. "I'll be there in a minute."

Rebecca followed the woman, in awe of her surroundings, amazed that it wasn't as foreboding as she'd imagined and feeling even more embarrassed that he felt he had to look after her. She didn't want to be a bother.

"You brought her *here*?" she heard a woman say.

"Keep your voice down," Aaron said. "She could hear you."

"But why didn't you just take her back to her room?"

"Because I didn't think it would be appropriate for me to spend the night in one of the guests' bedrooms."

"You could have just asked one of the staff to stay with her. You didn't have to look after her yourself. You should have convinced her to go to the hospital."

"She doesn't like hospitals, and she's one of our guests. Besides, it shouldn't have happened."

"Oh, Aaron," a younger female said. "You're such an old man. Things like this happen all the time."

"All our guests should be safe. I knew those party boats would be a problem."

"What are you so worked up about? They're not even part of our business. If she wants to sue, she can sue them—what happened has nothing to do with us. You always take on more responsibility than necessary. Send her home."

"Not until I'm sure she's okay. I just wanted you to know why she's here, not for you to try to change my mind."

"Well, you certainly need to change your clothes," the older woman said. "You're dripping water everywhere."

He snapped his fingers. "Oh, right, she needs clothes. Candace, could you give her something?"

"Aaron," the older woman said, irritated. "Just have the staff go to her room and get some of her things."

"Mum, it'd take too long. She could catch a chill and get sick."

"What chill? It's perfectly warm, and I doubt she's that delicate," the younger woman added. "You're such a protector."

"I don't have time for this. I have to go change and then keep an eye on her. Will you help me or not?"

"Okay, just this once."

Rebecca pretended to watch TV when she heard his footsteps. He stopped and looked in on her. "Why aren't you sitting down?"

"I didn't want to get the sofa wet."

"Right, I'm sorry," he said, looking contrite. "I forgot about that. My sister will have something for you to wear in a minute. I'm just going to get changed, and I'll be right back."

"You really don't—" she started, but he'd left before she could finish.

Rebecca looked around the elegant room, feeling even more awkward than before. If his family didn't want her there, maybe she should have gone to the hospital. She felt fine. She wasn't nauseous and was steady on her feet, and she didn't like feeling like a stray cat he'd found.

She put his jacket down, then poked her head out into the hallway. No one was around, and if she left, then the problem would be solved. She started to tiptoe to the doorway when she heard an amused female voice. "That's not a good idea."

She turned around and saw an attractive young woman, a little older than Aaron, grinning at her. "He'll just come and find you." She held out several clothing items. "Just get changed, and get used to being here."

"But I'm really okay," Rebecca said, reluctantly taking the clothes.

"My brother takes his responsibilities seriously," the woman said, leading Rebecca to a bathroom. "He's going to look after you until the morning, so you might as well get used to the idea. I'm Candace, by the way. If you haven't figured it out by now, my family owns the hotel where you're staying."

"Rebecca," she said, following the woman's example. Rebecca walked into the bathroom, then turned to her. "This is all so embarrassing."

"Embarrassing? You have no idea how many girls would love to be in your shoes." She winked and then closed the door.

Resigned, Rebecca changed, then looked at her torn dress. She'd designed it herself, but the stitching hadn't been strong enough. She'd have to take better care in the future. She didn't want them to think she'd fallen overboard on purpose. Then her thoughts turned back to her rescuer. He was wonderful, and she could understand why he'd be a hot catch, but she didn't want to give him or his family the wrong impression. But since she was going to have to stay, she decided she'd make the best of it.

In truth, she was curious to know more about him and wanted to spend as much time with him as she could. Once she put on the skirt and top Candace had handed her, she looked in the mirror and wasn't too surprised by the image she saw. She looked terrible. While the skirt and top would look stunning on the other woman's tall willowy frame, Rebecca looked awkward and dumpy because she was almost a foot shorter and a little wider.

But she was used to wearing secondhand clothes, and as a fashion major she knew that clothes could be made to fit the woman. She rolled up the skirt at the waist, so it fell shorter, just above her knees. Then she folded up the arms of the top and pulled and tied it in the back, then looked at her reflection, satisfied. She heard a quick knock on the door. "Can I come in?" Candace asked.

"Yes."

Candace came in holding a bottle in one hand and a hair dryer in the other. She stopped and stared at her. "Wow, I've never seen those items worn like that before."

Rebecca shrugged. "I had to make some adjustments, but don't worry, none of the changes are permanent."

Candace walked around her, impressed. "Very

creative." She set the hair dryer and bottle of moisturizer down. "I thought you might want this for your hair."

"Thanks." Once Candace left, Rebecca plugged in the blow dryer, then lathered her bare skin with some of the moisturizer. She had exchanged her heels for a pair of plush slippers once she had entered the house and felt more comfortable. Before leaving the bathroom, Rebecca checked her reflection. With the help of the blow dryer, her hair looked slightly tamed, and she had wiped off her smudged makeup. That would have to do, she thought with a shrug, then left. She found Aaron sitting in front of the TV dressed in khaki pants and a T-shirt. When he turned and looked at her, he stood up and smiled. "Now you look much better."

Rebecca looked down at herself. "Liar."

He rested his hand on his chest as if she'd wounded him. "Why would I lie?"

"Because you're sweet."

He winced. "Ouch, you really know how to hurt a man's ego. You want the truth?"

"I didn't say that."

He handed her a phone. "Here."

"What's that for?"

"In case you want to call someone and let them know you're okay."

"Oh, right," she said, taking the phone. "Thanks." She dialed her friend Marie and told her what had happened.

"You really should go to the hospital," Marie said after Rebecca had finished. "I heard something bad happened on that boat."

"Shh, I'm all right," Rebecca said, wishing that Marie didn't have a habit of shouting over the phone.

"Who is this guy? What if he made up his story about chaperoning the boat and plans to take advantage of you?"

Rebecca glanced over at Aaron, who continued watching TV, hoping he couldn't overhear her friend. "I've already met his sister, and his mother's here, too," she said in a low voice, hoping Marie would take a hint and do the same. "Nothing's going to happen."

"But what if they're not really related to the owners, and they're a group of cons who prey on tourists and—"

Rebecca inwardly groaned, regretting her choice to call. Maybe she should have told her a different story. Marie had a wilder imagination than she did. "I'm okay. The reason I called you was so that you *wouldn't* worry. I'll see you in the morning."

"Just remember that if he tries anything, go for the soft spots and—"

"Good night," Rebecca said before disconnecting. She handed the phone back to Aaron, then sat down.

Aaron replaced the phone and sat beside her. "What soft spots should you go for?"

Rebecca felt her face burn. "You heard that?"

"Couldn't help it. I think I could hear your friend over a hurricane warning."

"She just worries sometimes."

Aaron nodded, then pointed to the TV. "You can watch whatever you want."

"I don't watch much TV," Rebecca said, glancing around the room. She pointed to a covered table near the wall where a framed item sat. She saw a miniature three-dimensional scene of people taking a picture in the cove. "What's that?"

"Oh, just one of my hobbies."

She walked over to it. "It's beautiful. What is it called?"

"A diorama."

"Do you have others?"

Aaron looked at her, skeptical. "You really want to see them? My job is to keep you awake, not put you to sleep."

"I won't fall asleep. I'm really curious."

"Okay." He lifted up the tablecloth and set three more dioramas on the table.

Rebecca bent down and studied their intricate details.

"I base some of them on stories like *Treasure Island* or *Robinson Crusoe*, but I mostly like showing scenes of nature," Aaron said after a while, as if he was made uncomfortable by her silence.

She turned to him. "You really love this island, don't you?"

"It's my life."

"You remind me of my grandmother."

Aaron frowned and started to put the dioramas away, annoyed. "Because this is the hobby of an old woman?"

"No, because you create beautiful things. My grandmother is one of the most amazing women I've ever known. I'm a fashion design major because of her. She couldn't afford much, but she always made me look and feel good. Even when other kids would make fun of a sweater she created, I didn't care, because every time I put something on that she made, I knew I was loved. She'd take my sister and me to the park and just look at birds, and gain inspiration for a dress or blouse. She'd race home and gather different cloths and materials and create something amazing. She lives life with passion. Just like you."

"No one has ever said that to me before. I'm not really—"

"But you are," Rebecca interrupted. "Looking at what you've created makes me want to be an inch tall so that I can escape into this world. I can see your love of this island and the people here. You're so talented. I wish I could create something this intricate."

"They are really not that difficult to make. It just takes some patience. Want me to show you?"

"Yes."

All through the night Aaron eagerly showed Rebecca his collection of art materials and selection of intricate hand tools he used, and walked her through the basic steps to making a diorama. Then they spent the rest of the time sharing their hopes and dreams.

He told her about his vision to expand his family's hotel into an international holiday resort; she told him how she hoped to travel the world and become a famous designer one day. She made him laugh with her imitations of her various college roommates and professors, and her grandmother.

"I know your mother died in a hospital, but what about your father?" Aaron finally asked. "You only talk about your grandmother."

"He's gone, too. He died when I was three. But don't feel sorry for me. My grandmother and sister love me enough for both my parents."

Aaron pressed the back of his hand against her forehead. "How do you feel?"

At that moment she felt hot, but not from illness. She adjusted her position and moved out of his reach. "Good. I was sleepy before, but now I'm having so much fun, I'm not even thinking about what happened."

He looked at the small scene she was completing, which consisted of a palm tree and what looked like a baby seal, sunning on a beach.

"It's not very good," she said. "But at least I've enjoyed making it ."

"You're doing a great job, and it's almost morning so I think you'll be safe."

"You want me to go now?"

"No, not yet," he said with a smile. "I just didn't want you to be worried about having to stay here too much longer."

"Why not? I like it here. You're fun."

He laughed.

"What's so funny?"

"No one has ever said that to me, either. You really are a strange one."

"How can that be strange? You are fun."

He leaned in and kissed her on the forehead. "Thanks, I really needed to hear that. You're sweet." He stood. "Let me go get us something to eat."

When Aaron returned carrying a large tray filled with bowls of fruit, hot cereal and toast, she could hardly eat. She couldn't focus. He'd kissed her. Sure, it was on the forehead and like a kiss a big brother would give a little sister, but that didn't matter. He'd kissed her.

He'd not only saved her life and listened to her stories, he made her feel special. No one had ever made her feel that way before.

Chapter 4

Rebecca returned to her hotel room madly in love. Over the next three days, she saw him around the hotel, but except for a casual nod, she didn't catch his attention, even though she tried. She took great pains to make sure her hair was styled and her makeup was done right, and dressed up in her most attractive outfits. When another recent attempt failed, Rebecca sat and watched him from a distance.

"Stop that," Marie said as the two lounged in an outdoor café.

Rebecca looked at her friend, surprised. Marie had a face as exciting as wet cardboard and an attitude to match, but Rebecca liked her anyway. "What am I doing?"

"Sighing. Whoever he is, he's not interested. Forget about him."

"Why?"

"Because he's completely out of your reach. Besides, he probably has his pick of women anyway. Why would he choose you?"

"I say you should go for it," Candace said, coming up to sit at their table.

"Why?" Marie challenged, looking at the woman with suspicion.

Candace shrugged. "Why not?"

"Why don't *you* go for him?" Marie asked.

Candace made a face. "Because he's my brother, and that would just be gross."

"Marie, this is Candace," Rebecca said, making the introductions. "Candace, Marie." After the two women shook hands, Rebecca said, "You really think I have a chance with Aaron?"

"Yes." Candace looked over Rebecca's dress. "Did you make that?"

"Yes."

"I like your style. You've got a great eye for color." She grinned. "You know I like you, and I want to help you."

"Help me?"

"Yes. To get my brother. He needs someone like you."

Rebecca leaned in closer with hope and longing. "Really?"

"Yes." She lowered her voice. "He's just getting over a really bad breakup and has been miserable. She was awful to him, but that night you were with him, you made him smile, and that's not easy to do. Actually, we're all worried about him."

"Worried?"

"He really loved the other woman, and he may do something reckless. I think you'll help him forget her. They'd been together two years, and she never once told him she loved him. He's aching for a woman to tell him that."

Rebecca felt her heart racing. She hated the thought of Aaron being sad or someone hurting him. She'd do whatever it took to make him smile again. She knew he was the one for her. "Tell me what I can do."

"I don't like this," Marie said the next evening as she sat on her bed and watched Rebecca put on her lipstick.

"You've already said that ten times."

Marie drew up her legs and rested her chin on her knees. "How do you know you can trust her?"

Rebecca put her lipstick away. "She's been nice to me, and why wouldn't you believe her?"

"Because she's beautiful. Beautiful women don't know what it's like for the rest of us, and they can't be trusted."

"You sound jealous."

"I'm not really. I'm just worried about you."

Rebecca sat on the bed and patted Marie on the head the way she would an affectionate pet. "You're always worried about me. But don't be. He's the one. I know he is."

"I've never seen you like this."

"I know," Rebecca said, as surprised as her friend about how strong her feelings were. "That must mean something. I have this feeling that I have to be with him. When I first saw him, I felt this connection."

"That's only because you were filled with fear. It was probably just a regular chemical reaction."

Rebecca shook her head. "No, it wasn't that. It was something more. I can't put how I feel into words." She jumped to her feet, then slowly spun around with her arms held out to the sides. "How do I look?"

"Can I be honest?"

Rebecca stopped turning and let her arms fall. "Do you have to be?"

"Yes."

Rebecca folded her arms and braced herself for her friend's criticism. "Then go on."

"You're going to get hurt. Not only that, you're going to be humiliated. Girls like us don't get men like Aaron Wethers."

"Are you finished?"

"Yes."

Rebecca held her arms out again. "Okay, now how do I look?"

Marie rolled her eyes and fell back on the bed. "Did you hear a word I said?"

"Yes, but you haven't answered my question."

"It doesn't matter what you look like," she said, looking up at the ceiling.

"Yes, it does."

Marie sat up with a frown. "You look great."

"Thanks," Rebecca said, grabbing her purse and heading for the door.

Marie pointed at her and said in a grim voice, "Just don't say I didn't warn you."

Rebecca looked at the note and map Candace had given her. She was supposed to go to a cliff that overlooked a private grove where Aaron liked to be alone. The early-evening sun painted the sky purple and red, and the breeze fingered the blue ocean. Rebecca didn't see him at first, taken in by the beauty around her. She could understand why he'd love going to this spot. She could see so much potential for the creative mind. Then she saw him staring straight ahead, looking at the crashing waters below, his hands in his pockets. Her damaged hero looked so alone. Then he took his hands out of his pockets and started walking toward the edge of the cliff. Her heart stopped, and she drew in her breath.

"No!" she screamed, then ran and tackled him to the ground.

"Are you out of your mind?" he yelled, shoving her off him with such force that Rebecca's head hit the ground hard.

"No, you are," Rebecca said, sitting up. "But it's okay now." She touched the back of her head, then looked at her hand and saw blood.

He swore. "Oh, it's you. Wait. Hold still," he said, and before she could argue, he ran his hand over her head, looking for the source of the bleeding. "It's a small cut, but it should be cleaned." He sat back on his heels and glared at her. "You're a walking disaster."

"I wouldn't have gotten hurt if you hadn't been so reckless. What are you doing?" she asked when he pulled off his T-shirt.

"Applying pressure," he said, pressing his rolled-up shirt to the back of her head. "Hold it there for a minute." He took her hand and placed it on the shirt. "And I don't know what you're talking about. I'm never reckless."

"You were standing on the edge of a cliff ready to jump to your death."

He pointed to himself. "Me?"

"Yes, no woman is worth throwing away your life. You have too much to live for."

He frowned, then sniffed her. "Funny, you don't smell drunk."

"I'm not."

"Don't you know this is a private area?"

"I came to see you." She took his hand with her free one. "I'm glad I did. I'm here for you."

He pulled his hand away. "Are you on something?"

"No, but you can trust me. I know you're hurting. Your sister told me about your breakup and—"

"Oh, so my sister put you up to this? You think this is funny?"

"No. You saved my life, and I'm willing to save yours."

He stood, then pulled her to her feet. "I wasn't trying to kill myself. Diving off that cliff always helps to clear my thoughts."

"But you're wearing your street clothes. If you're planning to swim, shouldn't you be wearing trunks or something?"

Aaron lifted a brow. "You're lucky I didn't decide to dive in the nude. I like to do that, too." He bent her head forward and checked her cut. "It's stopped bleeding, thank goodness," he said with a smile, then turned. "Do you want an ice cream cone?"

"I love you."

He spun around, his eyes blazing. "What did you just say?"

"I love you," Rebecca repeated, her insides trembling.

"You love me?" he said, his tone as hard as steel.

"Yes."

"I thought you were different, a crazy little mouse, but I liked you." He shook his head, amazed. "You really had me fooled."

"Fooled?" she said, confused by his anger. "It's the truth. I think—"

He rested his hands on his hips and looked at her in disgust. "Do I look so pathetic that I need a child to make me smile?"

"I'm not a child."

"You're right, a child is innocent and you're not." He turned and started walking away.

She grabbed his arm. "Aaron, wait."

He seized her shoulders. "This is my last warning. Don't touch me again—don't even breathe my name. You disgust me." He shoved her away, then headed to his house.

Rebecca crumpled to the ground and watched him walk away, tears streaming down her face, heartbroken. She disgusted him? The man she loved, the man she'd tried to rescue, didn't even want her to touch him or say his name? His disdain had ripped her heart in two, exposed all her insecurities and vulnerabilities. It reminded her that she'd been raised by a poor grandmother who'd had to work two jobs to get by, that she'd been eighteen when she'd bought her first new dress instead of one that had been used. Aaron Wethers was definitely out of her reach.

Rebecca rose to her feet and slowly walked to the cliff, the waters below calling to her, tempting her to ease her pain forever. Marie had been right. She'd ended up heartbroken. She hadn't expected him to be like that. She'd thought he'd liked her, too. Why did her expression of love make him change? Did he think she was unworthy of loving him?

She'd thought he was different. She didn't think he'd dismiss her as if he were lord of the manor, and she was one of the servants. He'd been sharp but kind to her before. But this time, she felt the biting cruelty of his words. All that she'd imagined him to be was wrong.

Girls like us don't get men like Aaron Wethers, Marie had said. Rebecca wiped her tears with the back of her hand, then gripped her hands into fists as she stared at the blue waters below. For a moment, he'd made her feel like dying, but her life meant something, too.

That's when she decided that one day, she'd have men like Aaron chasing after her.

Ten years later, Rebecca remembered the young woman she used to be with pity. She'd been naive to believe that Aaron Wethers had been The One. She looked out at the ocean from her villa. He was still charming and considerate as any owner would be, but she wouldn't be fooled by that. Besides, any interest from him after he figured out who she was would be anticlimactic and show her how shallow he really was. He'd be like all the other men she'd met who were interested only in her fame, her money and her looks. Of course, turning him down would still be fun. She'd enjoy rejecting him. Maybe she could toy with him a little before she did, and remind him of his own cruelty to her ten years ago.

Rebecca smiled at the thought, then frowned. First she had to save her show. But why did his eyes still draw her to him? Why did his touch still make her tremble? Why did she still see the damaged hero that she'd imagined him to be ten years ago? She shook her head and turned from the ocean view. She couldn't afford to be that fanciful or foolish. Her show was at risk.

This collection was important to her. She'd worked hard to get to this moment. She'd studied in New York and London, having her first show at twenty-three before partnering with her ex—a musician whose style she'd invented and created an immediate fashion trend that had exposed her. She expanded from men's wear into women's fashion, and her work was quickly snatched up by boutiques—growing her business faster than she could have expected. She'd come to St. James expecting to see Aaron again, this time as a global success—expecting to be the one in control.

But her heart made her doubt that she'd ever be in control where he was concerned.

Chapter 5

Harvey left his aunt's house with a plastic smile and her voice ringing in his ears, after twenty minutes of begging him to find a bride, when he saw a familiar figure marching down the street in a place she didn't belong. It was Rebecca Cromwell in a strange disguise. She was wearing a large hat and dark glasses.

It was a dangerous part of town, and tourists shouldn't wander through it. But she looked as if she knew where she was going. He followed her and saw her disappear into a house ten minutes later.

Once she came out of the house, he approached her. "Miss Cromwell, you shouldn't be here."

She stopped and stared at him, startled. "You know who I am?"

"Of course I do," he said, finding her question odd.

She blinked, suddenly afraid. "And you followed me?"

"I was worried about you."

She glanced around in a furtive manner, then said, "Nobody can know I was here. You can't mention it to anyone, please. Don't even bring it up when you see me again."

"I won't, but—"

"Thank you."

"But if you're in trouble—"

"I'm not, I just had some business I needed to take care of."

"Let me escort you back to the—"

"I really could use something to eat. Do you know of a place?"

"Not around here."

"I don't want to eat at the resort. I like to be around the regular people sometimes. Where's your favorite place?"

"It's nothing remarkable—just a little jerk chicken stand."

"Sounds wonderful."

Minutes later, they stood near Bawley's Jerk Favorites. "What would you like?"

"Just order what you like."

He'd never had to do that. He was a man who lived alone and rarely went out on dates. Harvey suddenly felt unsure. He had a desire to please her, but he liked his food spicy and didn't know her tastes. He pulled out his handkerchief.

She laughed.

He turned to her, confused.

"You don't have to be so nervous. It's not like you're ordering for the queen."

"I like my food spicy."

"Me, too." She playfully nudged him with her elbow.

"And I'm starving, so hurry up and order something before I faint."

Harvey felt himself relax and stepped up to the food stand, where a man with a multicolored hat and conch shells necklace grilled. When he glanced up and saw Harvey, he grinned. "It's been a while. Boss man keep you dancing?"

"Yes, it's been busy. I'd like to order two of your jerk chicken."

"I'm not sure I heard you properly. Did you say two?"

Harvey sighed, knowing what would come next. "Yes."

He looked past Harvey at Rebecca. "She's yours?"

"Of course she's not mine. She's a guest at the resort."

"You never bring guests here. She must be someone special. Don't worry, you know that my special spice can make any woman fall in love."

Harvey couldn't help but laugh. Edmund Brawley was a man known for his way with women.

"Fine, as long as you don't charge me extra."

"She doesn't look to be from around here."

"Have you got cotton in your ears? I said she's a guest."

"Oh, right. One of those fancy women from the resort just happened to find her way over here."

"It can happen."

"It hasn't happened before. They're too high to mingle with the locals. Is she British?"

"American."

"Pity."

"Pity?"

"Them women be hard. Before you know it, you'll find yourself wearing a pinny and cooking her breakfast before she goes off to work."

"There's nothing wrong with a woman working," Harvey said, knowing *pinny* was slang for *pinafore*.

"I didn't say that. Did you hear me say that? I'm just saying that they can be hard, so you have to be even harder or they'll take your balls and—"

"You done yet?"

"Almost."

"We're not all like that," came a female voice from behind him.

Harvey spun around. "Food is almost ready."

"It's much more interesting standing here. I couldn't help overhearing you two."

"It's better to just eat his food and ignore everything else he says."

"What was her name?" Rebecca asked.

Edmund looked up at her. "Who?"

"The American who broke your heart."

He started to grin. "Who says there was only one?"

Harvey said, "If you're not done, we're going somewhere else."

"Okay, okay, dancing man. He's always in a hurry because he works for the Wetherses. Hardly can get H.C. to stand still."

Harvey paid for the food, then escorted Rebecca to a spot looking out at the water. "I hope you weren't offended by what he said."

"Not at all. What does H.C. stand for?"

"Just my initials. I prefer it to my given name."

"Which is?"

"Better left unsaid."

She laughed. "Point taken." She bit into the succulent chicken leg. "Mmm...this is delicious. I'll have to come back here before I leave."

"Let me know when, and I'll bring you. It's not safe for you to be here alone."

"How come a man like you hasn't been snatched up yet?"

Harvey felt his face grow warm. He'd never had someone ask him that before, besides his aunt. People rarely saw past Wethers to see him. But because she wasn't from the island, she didn't know that.

"No time."

"You should steal time, like this."

She smiled, and he felt his heart melt. Her friendly, open nature wasn't what he'd expected from a successful top designer used to being surrounded by beautiful people. He liked her, a lot. He knew she was out of his league, but that didn't matter. Making her show a success had now become a personal mission.

Rebecca Cromwell. Aaron sat in his office and stared at his laptop, unable to focus. Why did her name seem to mean something to him? Not because she was a known designer—he didn't follow that world enough to make her name important to him. There was something else. Something familiar about her. Something about her face that had shifted his sleeping heart. Her wild halo of black curls, which surrounded her delicate yet impish features, made him think of the playful energy of a wood nymph.

He'd been with Martha for two months now, and she'd never made him feel this way, this restless and eager for more. And he would bet Rebecca had been naked under her robe. He'd already imagined her in the buff more than he should have, and he wanted to see her again, even though he knew he shouldn't. She was exactly the kind of woman he'd vowed to stay away from, but that hadn't stopped him from calling the maître d' so that he would be alerted the moment anyone used one of his "special" cards.

Rebecca Cromwell. She'd turned a moment that could have been a PR nightmare into a comical farce. Aaron couldn't help smiling, remembering her fake greeting and clever idea to disguise Trident in the laundry cart to get him out of her villa without anyone knowing. He liked her spunk and cunning. And her looks—he couldn't pretend that he hadn't gotten a whiff of her intoxicating scent when she'd crashed into him. Although, as he'd held her, he could feel her trembling. She smiled and laughed as if she weren't afraid. When she'd hugged him, he'd had to stop himself from holding her a second longer, just to calm her.

He wanted to get to know her better. He hadn't felt that way about a woman in a long time. And she'd been kind to Brandon. He could imagine another guest scolding him, and they'd be right to. But instead, she'd left that job to him. He appreciated that. Being a single father was hard enough without others telling him what he was doing wrong. His cell phone buzzed, and when he looked at it he saw a message from H.C. that security was ready to talk.

Aaron met with his security staff and learned that their mood was still strong, despite the mishaps. No one else seemed as concerned as his sister. They answered all of Aaron's questions with rational replies, but agreed they'd increase their efforts to make sure nothing else went wrong. But as much as they assured him and told him their strategy, something still needled him.

"Tell me the true story," he said to Brandon while they ate dinner that night.

"What?"

"About Trident. I told that ridiculous story about the villa being aired out to Ms. Cromwell for appearances, but we both know that's never happened before. What really happened?"

"I told you. I don't know. I let him go free just a minute, and then he was gone."

"Iguanas don't just disappear. And someone would have seen him. He's old and he's big. He's hard to miss."

"I know, Dad, but I'm telling you the truth. Honest," he said, an anxious note in his tone, his eyes pleading for understanding.

"I believe you," Aaron said, and his son smiled. He was glad the tension between them was gone, but that didn't ease his mind. Something was going on, and he had to find out what. For some reason, the iguana incident bothered him more than anything else.

"I'm glad she didn't shout at me. I hate when people shout."

"Hmm."

Brandon pushed the food around on his plate.

"If you're finished, you're excused, but don't play with your food."

Brandon shoved a mouthful of black beans and rice in his mouth, then mumbled something.

Aaron sighed. "Do you want to spend time with Nan learning table manners?"

Brandon shook his head, his eyes wide.

"Then don't talk with your mouth full, and take your time to eat. I'm not going anywhere."

Brandon quickly swallowed, then said, "Did you get to ask her?"

"Ask who what?" Aaron asked, feigning ignorance. He knew exactly who his son was referring to.

"The iguana lady."

"We have an iguana lady?"

"Come on, Dad, I'm serious."

"So am I. I'm a busy man. I deal with a lot of people. What's the iguana lady's name?"

Brandon gave a heavy sigh. "Ms. Cromwell."

"What about Ms. Cromwell?"

"Is she married?"

Aaron shrugged. "I don't know."

Brandon gaped at him, stunned. "You didn't ask her?"

"I told you I wouldn't."

"I thought you might have changed your mind."

"I didn't."

Brandon fell silent a moment, then his face brightened. "I don't think she's wearing a ring, so that means she's not, right?"

"She probably has a boyfriend."

His face fell. "Really?"

"Yes, really."

He bit his lip, then said, "Probably doesn't mean for sure, right?"

Aaron nodded to his son's plate, ready to change the subject. "Finish your dinner."

"I like her, Dad."

"You only just met her. You don't know anything about her."

"I know that she's pretty and funny and—"

"She's leaving the island in less than two weeks. Now finish your dinner."

Brandon set his fork down. "I'm done," he said, then took his plate and utensils over to the sink. "And I still like her," he called out before he raced up the stairs.

Aaron hid a smile and softly said, "I like her, too."

And that evening while he dreamed, Aaron did a lot more than just like her. He held her and kissed her and got to see what she had hidden under her robe. He saw her bare brown body tangled in his sheets and then tangled around him, his hands exploring the soft satin of her skin while he felt the weight of her legs wrapped around him. She whispered his name and cried out in pleasure. He woke up the next morning as hard as sugarcane with a smile on his face, until his phone alert reminded him he had plans to take Martha out for lunch. *Martha.* He was seeing Martha. That was the woman who should have been in his dream. She was the woman he'd considered marrying. He groaned. He needed a cold shower.

But the stinging cold drops of water on his skin did nothing to cool his thoughts. "She's all wrong for you," he mumbled to himself as he changed. He had to be sensible and reasonable. It was this kind of wayward thinking that had gotten him in trouble with Ina. "And she's leaving soon. Focus on the show and nothing else."

He repeated that mantra as he drove to the high school where Martha taught. He parked his car and decided to walk to the back of the school, where the teacher's lounge was, instead of driving there. Through one of the open windows, he saw Martha talking to a colleague and was about to announce himself when he heard her say, "Don't worry, Aaron Wethers will be putting a ring on my finger before the end of the year."

Aaron moved out of sight and leaned in to listen.

Her companion laughed. "You sound sure about that."

"Men like Aaron are so predictable about things like that. He wants a mother for his son, and I'm the perfect candidate. To be honest, his kid is the most interesting thing about him."

"That's mean," the other woman replied.

Martha giggled. "You're right, his money helps, too."

"I'm sure he's not that bad. Everyone likes him."

"He's a good guy, but let me just say, I know why his first wife left him. He looks like this handsome, romantic guy but he's nothing like his ancestor." She lowered her voice. "He's a little scarier."

"Scarier?"

"Yes, I don't know what it is, but sometimes when he looks at me I just want to run."

"And you still want to marry him?" her companion asked, surprised. "Are you afraid he's going to hurt you?"

"No, it's nothing like that. It's just that, at times, he's so intense, so virile it can feel overwhelming, and I hate when he asks me to come by the main house at night. I swear I once heard the sound of a machete tapping against a post."

"Then how will you stand living there?"

"I'll find a way, and besides, it makes my mum happy. He's still a great catch, and I'm ready to be a mother. I hope to have a little brother or sister for Brandon within a year of marrying him."

Aaron came around the corner and sat down in an empty chair. "Shame that's not going to happen."

Both women jumped.

"Aaron," Martha gasped, covering her mouth.

He looked at Martha in her simple cotton dress and strict hairstyle. She was a vast contrast to Rebecca, whose wild hair would rebel against such a conservative bun and whose body could make a plain robe look sexy. "Did I surprise you? I guess scary guys can have their moments."

"That's not what I meant," Martha said in a rush. "You misunderstood. Let's talk about this later."

"What is there to talk about?"

"I don't know what you overheard." She stood close to him, gently touching his arm.

"Enough to know how you feel about me. Or rather, about my money and my son."

"I care about you, too. It's just—" She stopped and looked away.

"It's just what?" he pressed.

Martha looked at him, and her eyes filled with tears. "You're so hard to read."

He leaned forward, his dark gaze holding hers. "And that's what frightens you?"

"You're not like other men," she said, staring back at him with wide eyes. "You're so controlled. I never really know how you feel about anything, even me. I know you took me out and showered me with gifts, but you never once kissed me."

He stood and lifted her to her feet. She stiffened. "That's why," he whispered in her ear.

"What?"

He released her. "That's why I never kissed you. Every time I came toward you, you did that. You either stiffened or drew away. I thought I was being considerate by not rushing you."

"No," she said, lightly touching his sleeve before he could turn. "I was just nervous."

"And you're still nervous?"

She glanced at her friend, who looked at them, both mesmerized and confused, then met his gaze. "No, I'm not," she said, hugging herself.

"You're lying," he said, a cynical grin touching his lips. "But that doesn't matter now."

"Please don't," she begged, grabbing the hem of his jacket when he turned.

"Keep your dignity and let me go," he said softly.

"I don't want to lose you," she said, tightening her grip. "I was wrong. I'm sorry. I didn't mean to hurt you. I want this to work. We are really good together. Let's try again."

"What for? You know why my first wife left me. I'm not going to give another woman the chance to do the same."

Aaron turned around and walked out of the room without another word, jumped in his car and left the school, unsure whether he should be angry, annoyed or amused. He'd been the perfect gentleman with her. What did she mean he was too hard to read? Ina had once said that to him, too, except with a laugh instead of tears.

You're a lot wilder than you think, Candace had told him. But he didn't know what that meant. At least now he wouldn't feel guilty about his waning feelings for Martha. His sister had been right. He had been settling, but he'd seen no harm in it. Passion had ruled him once, and he didn't want it to reign again. His love for Ina seemed to bring out only the worst in him. Aaron swore, then accelerated. His personal life had to be put on hold. He had to make sure that the fashion show didn't face any more troubles.

A half hour later, he entered the large exhibit hall where the fashion show was scheduled to be held. Whoever was in charge of decorations was an extremely skilled artist. The entire hall had been transformed to look like a magical wonderland, a paradise. Enormous, colorful set designs lined the entire hall, leading up to the stage, which was decorated with a series of silk, hand-embroidered curtains in an assortment of dazzling colors, depicting the theme of the show, which was called Loving Adventure. Off to the side, a series of brightly painted life-size whimsical creatures were being prepared and put into place. He knew Brandon would be thrilled to see what was going on, but he also knew he wouldn't be interested in seeing the fashion show itself. Down the middle of the expansive hall was the runway, covered with plush royal blue carpeting.

He saw Rebecca talking to one of the lighting crew. One of the volunteers went up to her and asked her a question, which she answered before moving to a stagehand and pointing to one of the decorations. She certainly was a busy woman, and he wondered where her assistant was. He walked to the stage, convincing himself he was just doing his job, although he knew he wanted to see her for completely different reasons.

"Looks good."

Rebecca turned at the sound of Aaron's voice, surprised to see him looking up at her from the front of the stage, his golden-brown gaze drawing her in. Her heart started racing immediately, and she cleared her throat to keep her voice from shaking. "I'm surprised to see you here."

"Just wanted to check on things."

Right, he was just doing his job, Rebecca quickly reminded herself. He hadn't come to see her. She had to be as professional as he was. "Nothing to worry about, thank goodness. Everything is set. There was one minor lighting issue, but it's being addressed."

"Good."

She folded her arms and grinned, unable to miss the polite tone in his voice. "You don't like it."

Aaron raised his brows, surprised. "I didn't say that."

"I can tell by your face. You think it's too much?"

He looked around and shrugged. "It's art."

Rebecca's grin widened. She liked how uncomfortable he looked, and she enjoyed teasing him. "You're good. I'm not sure if that's an insult or a compliment."

His voice lowered, and his gaze grew serious. "It's whatever you want it to be."

Rebecca squatted so that they were at eye level. She knew it was a dangerous move, but she couldn't resist it. "Just wait until you see the clothes. They will blow your mind."

Aaron took a step closer, his gaze dropping to her lips before returning to her eyes. "Promise?"

Her heart pounded in her ears, all other sounds and sights falling away, except for him. "Do you want a guarantee?"

"No, I—" he said, then his face changed. He grabbed her, lifted her off the stage and covered her body with his just as she heard a loud crash. She stood sheltered by his warm, strong embrace, but she still felt the force of the impact and saw debris flying past. An eerie silence fell before Aaron looked down at her, his eyes searching her face. "Are you okay?"

"I'm fine," she said, stunned. "What happened?"

"That's what I plan to find out," he said in a grim tone. He turned to the stage and swore.

Rebecca looked at the stage in shock. Broken glass and fragments from some of the large wooden rods that were holding up the expansive curtains lay scattered everywhere. One of the main painted panels that had been near the back of the stage had fallen and was completely torn, damaging the other panels when it fell. Rebecca stood paralyzed while Aaron marched over and talked to security and one of the stage crew. She could imagine what would have happened if he hadn't been there. But she didn't want to think about that. It was just another accident, right? Except now she wasn't so sure. They'd have to completely redesign most of the stage; there was no way they could get an exact replacement in time. There were only ten days before the show.

"Go home," Aaron said.

She gripped her hands into fists. Those were the last words she'd expected from him. "You want me to quit? I'm not going to cancel."

Aaron shook his head, looking chagrined. "Sorry, wrong choice of words. I meant, go back to your villa."

"Oh."

"I'll call you."

Rebecca nodded, then noticed the cut on his arm. "You're hurt."

He glanced down. "Damn glass." He removed a tiny shard from his skin. "Don't worry. It's nothing."

Rebecca winced when he removed a second piece. "You need to have it cleaned and bandaged right away." She pointed to a volunteer. "Get me a first-aid kit."

"I don't—"

She grabbed a chair. "Sit down."

"Rebecca—"

"Let me do this," she said when the volunteer handed her the kit. *I owe you my life—again. It's the least I can do.* "Your sister told me to take care of you." She opened a bottle of antiseptic and put some on a dry cotton ball, then cleaned the wound.

Aaron grinned. "My sister wouldn't say something like that."

"Why not?" Rebecca said, wrapping the bandage.

"Because she knows I can take care of myself. Always have, always will. My sister acts like my little sister most times. She doesn't worry about me."

"She did once, and I was foolish enough to believe her," Rebecca said under her breath.

"What?"

"Nothing."

"We've met before, haven't we?" He studied her face. "There's something familiar about you," he said in a low, husky tone.

"Yes, but that's ancient history," Rebecca said, determined not to be affected by his words or, even worse, by his tone, which seemed to lure her to lean in closer. She stood. "And now I have to figure out how I am going to remedy this disaster. Excuse me."

He grabbed her hand before she could leave. "You don't have to pretend that what just happened didn't frighten you."

Rebecca avoided his gaze, the heat of his hand against her skin making her stomach flutter. "It was just a stage malfunction," she said, keeping her voice even. She didn't want him to see how frightened she really was. How worried and afraid she was that she'd made a mistake in seeing him again. That he'd once again see her as a burden or someone to be pitied one moment, then tossed aside the next. She wanted him to see only her strength. "It would have been worse if this had happened during the fashion show," she added, trying to add a note of humor.

"No, it would have been worse if it had fallen on you."

"Oh, yes, that, too," she said, keeping her voice light, although his steady gaze made her voice waver. "But at least it didn't."

"So you're not worried?"

No, she was terrified. Terrified by her desire to have him wrap his arms around her again and shelter her from all her fears. Terrified by her longing to press her lips against his and taste the sweetness of his kiss. But what terrified her the most, as she boldly met his steady golden-brown gaze, was that she'd already fallen for him all over again, even though she was doing her best not to. "No."

"I am," he said in a flat tone, though his gaze grew more heated. "It's my job to make sure my guests are safe."

A guest. That's all she was to him, of course, and that's all she ever would be. "I'm not going to sue, if that's what you're worried about."

"No, that doesn't worry me. I—"

She pulled her hand free. "I really have to get back to work."

"You can't stay here."

She spun around and glared at him. "I have no intention of leaving. This show is going to be a success, and nothing is going to stop me." She pointed to the ground. "I have no plans of leaving this island until that happens. I'm not scared."

"I know," he said with a note of respect. "I meant, you can't stay in the exhibit hall."

"Oh," Rebecca said, feeling some heat steal into her cheeks, wishing she didn't keep jumping to the wrong conclusion with him. "I'll be in my villa," she said in a clipped voice, then walked away.

But when she got back to her villa, she couldn't work. Instead, she jumped on her bed and called her sister, Rachelle. "How's Gran?" she asked once her sister answered.

"What's wrong?"

"Why should anything be wrong?"

"Because you know that Gran's fine, and you should be too busy getting ready for your show to be worried about her anyway."

"Nothing's wrong," she said, hoping her lie sounded sincere. She squeezed her eyes shut against building tears. She didn't want to fall in love again. She didn't want to make the same mistake twice. "I was just checking in."

"You're lying. The last time you came back from that island you were depressed for days, but never told me why. And now I hear the same note in your voice."

She opened her eyes and rested her head against the headboard. "I may have to cancel my show."

"Why?"

"A lot of things have gone wrong."

"Can't you fix them?"

"I'm trying, but I don't know anymore," she said, letting her tears fall. "I can't afford to fail here. I can't let him see me as a failure."

"Who?"

She sniffed and wiped her eyes, annoyed that she'd let her true fear slip. "Just people."

"But you said 'him.'"

"I didn't mean anyone specific. I meant 'them.' Just those designers and critics who hate my work."

"Hmm," her sister said, sounding unconvinced. "It's just nerves, I'm sure. I know the show will be a success. The bigger the obstacle, the bigger the triumph, right?"

Rebecca managed a laugh. "Yes, that's right. What was that?" she asked when she heard an unfamiliar sound in the background.

"What was what?"

"I thought I heard a red-throated cokoboro bird singing." The bird was native only in the Caribbean and South America.

"Oh, it's just the TV."

"I'm amazed at how clear the connection is. You almost sound as if you were here."

Her sister laughed. "Stop making me jealous. I wish. I'm watching a nature show and preparing my favorite oven-baked catfish recipe so that I can pretend to be having as much fun as you. How is the resort? Is it the same as you remembered?"

Yes. She sighed. *And there are so many things I want to forget.* "It's beautiful, but I don't have time to truly enjoy it. Fortunately, one of the owners has been very resourceful, and he's helped a lot, but things have been stressful."

"I'll bet. What's he like?"

"There's not much to say."

"Which means the exact opposite. I want details."

"I didn't call to talk about him."

"It's not just the show that's worrying you, is it?"

"I don't know anymore. I guess I wanted to hear you say that everything will be okay."

"It will be okay. Your show will be sensational because you're amazing. We Cromwell women always are."

"Thanks," Rebecca said, feeling some of her courage return.

"And don't let him—whoever he is—break your heart this time."

Her sister knew her too well. Rebecca sighed. She couldn't fool her; she knew that her anxiety was about a man. But not just any man.

"I won't," she said, making her words sound like a vow.

Chapter 6

Aaron called Harvey and had him gather all the workers together. Once they were there, he pointed to the demolished set. "This is unacceptable. What happened?"

"It came loose," one of the workers said.

"I can see that," Aaron snapped. "My question is why?"

"We've looked it over many times and can't find a reason!" another worker shouted.

"Then you're not looking hard enough."

"But—"

Aaron rested his hands on his hips. "Did you feel an earth tremor that I missed?"

"No, sir."

"Then stop with excuses and find me a reason."

Another man stepped forward, clearly the leader of the group. "It was just an accident."

Aaron folded his arms. "Why are you doing that?"

"Doing what?"

"Handing me a reason to fire you? I don't mind mistakes, but I don't like people who don't take ownership. That's what leaders do. I don't want to hear the word *just* pass your lips again. Is that understood?"

"Yes, sir," the man said, taking a step back.

Aaron was about to dismiss the men when he saw one of the younger workers looking restless and anxious. "Do you have something to say?"

"He's a good leader, sir. And we all worked really hard on this. This is good work. The pay is great. We did our best."

"So why do you think this happened?"

"The rumors."

"That's enough," the leader said.

"What rumors?" Aaron asked.

"That the show is cursed," the young worker said. "That it's not meant to be."

Aaron looked around at the group. "How many of you believe that?"

They all raised their hands.

"Fine, you're dismissed. There's no need to return tomorrow." He turned and left.

Harvey followed him, running to keep pace. "Don't you think that's a bit harsh?"

"I don't have time to indulge in childish fantasies. Rebecca nearly got killed, and there's a rational reason for it. I don't have time to listen to superstitions or rumors."

Harvey pulled out his handkerchief and wiped his forehead. "But these men are some of our finest workers."

"They are also scared workers, and that makes them dangerous."

Harvey rubbed the back of his neck. "But to fire them—"

Aaron spun around and pinned him with a hard glare. "What would you have done with people who refuse to give you a reason for a major panel and support beams falling down? They're so busy defending themselves and worrying about their jobs that they're not thinking. Something went wrong, that's obvious."

Harvey hesitated, then dropped his gaze to the handkerchief in his hand. "Let me talk to them."

"Why?"

He lifted his gaze. "Someone may have seen something. You don't understand the dynamics."

Aaron frowned. "What dynamics?"

"People don't want to disappoint you. We look up to you, and nobody would want to admit that they've let you down. Let me find out what may have happened before you hire a new team."

Aaron sighed. H.C. had a point. He remembered how eager he'd been to please his father. He had to be logical, even though the thought of how close Rebecca had come to getting hurt still angered him. He remembered how she trembled in his arms, the look of fear on her face, although she struggled to hide it from him. If he wanted to keep her safe, he had to trust others, and H.C. was one of the men he trusted the most.

"You have three hours," Aaron said. Harvey nodded, then left. Aaron was headed back to his office when his cell phone rang. "Hello?"

"Someone is using your card in the VIP lounge," the maître d' said.

"Thanks." He hung up. That was faster than he'd thought. Especially after what had just happened. He'd thought Rebecca would be busy working the rest of the day, but now he had a chance to see her again, sooner than expected, and he wouldn't miss that opportunity.

You're a lot wilder than you think, his sister had said. Maybe it was time to find out how much wilder. He went into the lounge and had the maître d' point out where he'd placed her, but when Aaron walked up to the table, he knew it wasn't Rebecca, even from the back.

"May I?" he asked, gesturing to the empty chair.

"Please."

"Where's Ms. Cromwell?"

Kelli smiled with flirtation. "I don't know, but maybe I can help you."

"Where were you this afternoon?"

Her smile disappeared. "Why?"

"I didn't see you in the exhibit hall."

She lifted a sly brow. "Were you looking for me?"

"No, I just thought I'd see you there."

"I was there, but the moment you walked into the room, Rebecca was the only woman you saw."

"I can't deny it."

"Lucky you were there. I think she should cancel the show."

Aaron's jaw twitched. "I won't let that happen. This show will be a success, or do you doubt me?"

"No, that would be careless. I'd never underestimate you."

He leaned back. "Good."

"But I was shocked by what happened, so I had to get away. Rebecca's working, like always, and told me to enjoy this little treat instead."

"I see."

Kelli shook her head. "No, you don't. You might as well give up now. I can read people, and you're not her type."

"I suppose I'm yours," Aaron said as he slowly traced a circle on the white tablecloth.

She leaned forward. "How can you tell?"

He flattened his hand and smiled. "I can read people, too."

She rested her chin in her hand. "And what do you know about me?"

"You're the kind of woman who rarely eats alone."

"Food always tastes better with company."

"And you probably have a boyfriend at home who doesn't know that you like to keep company as often as you can."

Her eyes widened. "How did you...?"

"Know?" he finished for her with a grin. "I've met many different people here, and I can tell the ones who are coming for a little holiday fun. I know the ones who think that what they do here doesn't matter, as long as no one finds out. Let me guess...you've been with him over a year, yes?"

"It's nothing serious."

"I bet he thinks it is, or he wouldn't have bought you that bracelet. I couldn't help noticing the two hearts with the initials D.F. and K.D."

She covered her wrist. "He just likes to buy me things."

"Looks expensive." He studied her a little more. "He's about fifty, ready to settle down, sweet but not exciting, and he likes to take care of you. Has he brought up marriage yet? No? He will, and you know he will, and you'll consider it for the sake of security because you don't want to be some fashion designer's assistant all your life. But you're also young and want to be free. Am I close?"

Kelli folded her arms and glared at him. "You don't have to look so smug. You don't know all about me. I'm not a gold digger."

"No, you love him very much. So what game are you trying to play with me?"

Kelli held his gaze. She looked shaken, but she was not ready to admit defeat. "I have my own reasons."

"I'm sure you do, but I'm not in the mood to hear them." He stood. "Excuse me."

"Stay away from Rebecca," she said.

But she spoke with such venom that Aaron sat back down and looked at her with more interest. "Why?"

"Because she'll get hurt. You'll hurt her. Just like her ex-fiancé. He was gorgeous, sexy, a little dangerous... just like all musicians."

"You think I'm dangerous, too?" he asked in a low, deep tone.

"I know you are."

Aaron sniffed and looked at her with pity. "Whatever you've heard—"

"I don't have to hear anything. I know what men like you are about. If you really want to keep Rebecca safe, you'll tell her to leave this island."

He stood and pushed in his chair. "I have no intention of doing that. I'll make sure the show is a success."

"For her sake or yours?"

Aaron rested his hands on the table and stared down at her. "Do I look worried to you?"

"No," she said, lifting her glass and taking a sip. "Just a little overconfident." She set her glass down and held his steady gaze. "I know you think you can do a lot of things, but do you really think you can stop a curse?"

A *curse*. There was that damned word again, Aaron thought as he left the lounge. He should stop thinking about Rebecca. He knew Kelli was right. Rebecca had given his special VIP card away. That meant she had no interest in him. Then why did that intrigue him even more?

He saw her on the beach. At first she was just a silhouette in the dying light of the sun, but he could tell by her walk and confident, free-flowing movements that it was her. *Stay away from Rebecca,* Kelli had warned him. *I plan to do the exact opposite,* he thought as he made his way over to her.

"Hello," he said.

"Hi," she said, keeping her pace.

"Mind if I walk with you?"

"Yes."

He raised his brows, surprised. "Why?"

"Because then it will be very hard for me to ignore you."

"Why would you want to ignore me?"

"First, because I know how much you don't like the fashion world."

"That's true, but I'm willing to be tolerant, since I need to help your show succeed. H.C., my assistant, is talking to the crew, and we'll have a new one in if—"

"I don't want to talk about the show with you."

"Why not?"

"Because you broke my heart."

Aaron tapped his chest. "Me? Are you sure?"

She tilted her head at him. "You still don't remember me, do you? Have I really changed that much?"

"There is something familiar about you."

"Familiar, but not special, huh? I guess I shouldn't be surprised."

"Tell me how we met. Where."

Rebecca stopped walking and pointed to the water. "Out there."

"Out where?"

"In the ocean. Ten years ago, you saved me from drowning." She started walking again. "And when I offered my heart to you, you turned me away."

He blinked and didn't move. No, it couldn't be. "Becca? You're little Becca?"

She threw out her arms and kept walking, increasing the distance between them. "As you can see, I'm not little anymore. And I know it's best to stay away from you. You once called me a little mouse."

"I know," he said, walking up to her, easily closing the distance.

"Yes, but the little mouse now knows better than to play with the lion."

He shoved his hands in his pockets. "I didn't mean to hurt you—"

"What's past is past."

"And I don't see you as a mouse anymore."

She stopped and looked up at him. "I'm glad, because I want you to picture me as something else."

"What?"

"A dragonfly that you will never catch."

He shook his head. "I can't."

"Why not?"

"Because I have every intention of catching you," he said before his mouth covered hers.

Chapter 7

She wanted to pull away—her mind said she should, but her body didn't move from the sensual assault. Rebecca resisted slipping her arms around him, but she let her mouth taste the sweet corners of his lips and then his tongue. And when he drew her close, his hard form pressed against hers, she ached for more. He kissed her like a man claiming his possession. For those brief moments, he took ownership of her body in a way no man had. It surprised and aroused her. She wanted to be his. She always had.

She almost cried out in despair when he stepped back. The bond was still there, no matter how much she wanted to fight it. The bond they had developed that night all those years ago. But he hadn't felt it. He'd cast her aside, and she couldn't forgive him for that.

She folded her arms, trying not to tremble, desperate that he wouldn't see the effect he still had over her. "Finished having your fun?" she said, then lifted her hand to wipe his kiss from her lips.

He seized her wrist, stopping her. "Don't fight this, Becca."

She yanked her wrist free. "My name is Rebecca."

"I'm sorry about—"

She covered her ears and turned away. "I told you, what's past is past."

He grabbed her shoulders and spun her to face him, his gaze like summer lightning, his voice urgent. "You're smarter than that. Listen to me—"

She shirked away from him. "Stop, you're scaring me."

Aaron quickly released her and stumbled back as if she'd slapped him. "You don't mean that."

"I do. You're—"

He held up his hand. "No, you don't have to say it. Please don't say it. I can hear that from anyone but you." He turned and left, picking up a rock and throwing it in the water with anger.

Rebecca stared at him, regretting her reckless words, wondering why they had affected him so powerfully. Why they seemed to hurt him so much.

She pointed to his back as he became a smaller dot in the distance. *No, no, no, I'm not falling for it again. I'm not going to see you as the damaged hero who needs to be rescued. I'm wiser now. Smarter. I won't let you hurt me.* But even as she thought these words, she could feel tears stinging her eyes because she wanted to run after him and tell him that she wanted to be with him. That despite her greatest efforts to stop, she still loved him.

* * *

A few feet away, Harvey stared at her, feeling the force of his pain. Seeing Rebecca with Wethers had been a major blow. He hadn't expected that. When had that happened? Wethers usually kept a careful distance when it came to guests. Harvey knew that Rebecca couldn't be his, but he could imagine being with her. He'd already planned what he'd hoped to order for her next time he took her to his friend's jerk stand.

But Wethers had succeeded where he had failed. That was no surprise. She'd been kind to him, but he should not have mistaken her attention for attraction. Besides, Wethers was younger, with good looks and money. Of course she would choose him. Their parting didn't look cordial, however, and that gave him some hope. Although he had seen him kiss her, perhaps Wethers's advances were unwanted. And he knew why. He knew Rebecca's secrets.

As promised, he hadn't hinted at her secret meeting at the house in town. He'd barely spoken to her, knowing it best to keep his distance for her sake. But today she'd done something that bothered him and threatened everyone else. That's why he'd followed her to the beach. He'd come to talk to her about why she'd been lurking behind the stage a half hour before it collapsed. Was she behind what happened? There had to be a reason she'd been there, but why? Why would she sabotage her own show? He didn't know what to do. His first loyalty was to Wethers, but his heart cried out to protect her.

Should he tell Wethers his suspicions? Would he even listen to him? He had no proof, and it was all just speculation. Just because she'd been there didn't mean she'd done anything. She wouldn't try to hurt herself. Was it the curse? Rebecca seemed to be different when she was in the exhibit hall than when she'd been in town. What other secrets was she hiding?

You're scaring me. He never thought he'd hear those words from her, and they pierced his heart. He could take those words from Martha or Ina, but Becca had been different. She'd been one of the few people he'd felt most comfortable with. The one person who didn't make him feel as if he lived in the shadow of his ancestor, being compared to some of the wickedness Pierre LaCroix and his ancestors were known for. He had thought Rebecca was someone who didn't get caught up in talks of curses and superstition. A person who'd once made him laugh. Had she changed so much? And why did that thought hurt? He hadn't been looking for her. He never thought he'd see her again.

Aaron walked into his house, poured himself a drink and finished it in one swallow, letting the liquid heat burn his lungs. He probably should take a cold shower instead. Kissing Rebecca like that wasn't like him—he usually took his time, but he hadn't been able to resist. He'd planned to just tease her. Just a quick, light kiss to prove that she couldn't ignore him. But the moment his lips touched hers, something inside him leaped forth, transforming him from a man who prided himself on his restraint to a rogue who didn't give a damn. He devoured her, indulging in the heady sensation of her soft curves pressed against his body. It was only when he thought of taking her right there on the sand that he came back to his senses.

His father had raised him to be a gentleman, to be considerate. But he hadn't been; he'd cared only about the pleasure she was giving him, pleasure for which he'd been hungry for so long. He set his glass down. He'd once hurt her, and now she'd hurt him— fine cosmic justice.

He remembered with pain the young man he used to be. A young man who, at twenty-five, thought he knew all about life until he'd gotten his heart trampled on by his first love, Tonya. She'd been a popular radio announcer at their local station, and he'd been dating her for two years, with plans to marry her, when she'd called him to the station one night and demanded to know where their relationship was heading.

"What do you mean?"

"I mean, when do you plan to marry me?"

"My father's been ill, and I've had to take over some of his duties. When he's back on his feet we can talk about marriage."

"I don't want to talk about it. That's your problem, Aaron. You're always talking about things, or planning things, but you rarely do anything. Why don't we just elope?"

"You know I couldn't do that to my family."

"Don't you ever want to do something impulsive?"

"What's gotten into you?"

"I want to get married. I want to know where I stand with you."

"You know that I love you, but—"

"But what?"

"You've never once said that you love me." He'd

later regret baring his heart to her and saying those words when he learned she had deliberately kept the intercom on, and they'd been on the air, so his speech was heard by the entire island. Within minutes he was a running joke. He'd have cab drivers shout "I love you" as they drove by. Schoolgirls would say "We love you, Aaron" before laughing and running away. Ten years ago, he'd been a source of fun on the island, which was why he had tried to blend in with the college crowd that was staying at his family's hotel that spring break. At least none of them knew him or about his embarrassing declaration. He wanted to be seen as the proud owner of Red Beacon Hotel, not the pathetic, weak ex-boyfriend of a radio celebrity. His parents had been against the match in the first place, and her callous betrayal had proven them right.

"Focus on work. Everything will die down soon," his father said.

"I knew she was beneath you," his mother added.

He'd been remembering their discussion when he'd seen Rebecca go overboard. He had volunteered to go on the boat trip, since one of the chaperones had fallen ill earlier that day. He'd taken charge that night, organizing Becca's rescue. Taking her home had been a gamble, but he'd felt she was his responsibility, and he'd seen the respect in the EMTs eyes as well as the police officers, and craved it. He'd enjoyed being with her throughout the night, almost regretting when morning came and he had to send her home. He had wanted to show her some other sights on the island, but then thought better of it.

Two days later, he'd gone to his private place by the cliffs just to get away from another unfortunate meeting with his ex—and her new love—and try to forget the two groups of girls who'd shouted "I love you" when he had walked past. That evening, he'd planned on diving in the water, not caring about his clothes, when someone suddenly tackled him to the ground. He remembered Becca hitting her head and saying how she was trying to rescue him. He'd thought she was crazy but sweet, and after he'd checked her cut, he'd wanted to treat her to an ice cream cone and show her his progress on his latest diorama. But then she said those mocking words: *I love you.*

For a moment he couldn't believe the pain of her betrayal, almost more than the laughing look on Tonya's face. He'd been caught unawares; he'd never suspected that she'd laugh at him like all the rest. He'd stormed into the main house and was halfway up the steps when he bumped into his sister.

"You look like thunder," she said. "Where's your shirt?"

"I don't know," he said, walking past.

"What happened now?"

"Nothing."

"So you didn't see her?"

He gripped the railing and stopped. "See who?" he said softly.

"Never mind."

He turned around and grabbed her shoulder, forcing her to face him. "See who?"

"Becca."

"Why would I see Becca?"

"It doesn't matter if you didn't," Candace said, pushing him away.

"I did."

"Oh…then why are you so angry?"

He stared at her, outraged. "You're the one behind this?"

"Behind what? I was just trying to help. I know you like to go to that place alone."

"How many times have I told you not to mess with people's lives?"

"I thought she'd cheer you up."

"So you told her about Tonya and the radio show?"

"No, I didn't."

"Then why did you get her to say she loved me?"

Candace's mouth fell open. "I didn't expect her to do that. I told her—" She stopped and shook her head.

"You told her to do what?" he demanded.

"I told her I thought she'd be good for you. I could tell she really liked you, but I didn't expect her to say that."

"Then how did she know about the show? How did she know about what a joke I am?"

"I don't think she did. How could she? You know the island folk don't gossip with tourists. It's them versus us, you know that. They'd talk about you among themselves, but never shame you to an outsider."

She was right, and that's when the realization hit him. "That means she didn't know. She was saying the words for real. I didn't know she was saying the words and meant them."

"Oh, no. What did you say to her?"

He stared at his sister and swore, remembering his harsh words. He ran out of the house and rushed back to the cliffs, but by the time he got there, Becca was gone. He raised his arms above his head and yelled at the waves, now understanding the expression on her face. He thought she'd been acting, but now he remembered the shock on her face, the sheen of her eyes from the beginning of tears. Tears he'd caused. "Damn her!" He grabbed a fistful of earth and threw it over the side.

"Aaron?"

He spun around to see his sister. "Why did she have to say it like that? Why did she have to say it at all? I thought she was making fun of me like all the others." He lowered his gaze, his voice assailed by regret. "I hurt her, Candace. I didn't mean to hurt her like that. I wasn't myself, and I said things I shouldn't have."

"What did you say?"

"They were bad enough the first time. I'm not going to repeat them. Poor kid. I've got to talk to her."

"Where are you going?" she asked, grabbing his arm when he walked past.

"I have to apologize."

"You can't apologize like that."

"Like what?"

"You don't even have a shirt on."

"I'll get one."

"And second, it's kind of late to visit her room. She's not going anywhere. You can talk to her in the morning. Better yet, I will. I'll explain everything, since I'm partly to blame."

"No, I'll talk to her." He slapped his forehead. "I should have known when she tried to save me that she was being sincere."

"She tried to save you?"

Aaron sighed. "She thought I was going to jump off the cliff."

"But you do that all the time."

"She didn't know that."

Candace laughed. "She's such a romantic. Did you know she makes her own clothes?"

"She's definitely an interesting kid."

"I doubt she'd like to hear you say that."

"What? That she's interesting?"

"No, that she's a kid."

"She's too young for me, but I did consider her a friend. Fortunately, we can clear this all up in the morning."

But they never got the chance. Rebecca flew out early the next morning, and he'd thought he'd never see her again. How wrong he'd been.

She had every right to want to ignore him, but he would make that very hard. He'd make her regret the words she'd spoken and see him in a new way. After his divorce from Ina, he'd focused on his business and raising his son. But now Rebecca had given him a new focus. She reminded him that he was a man who didn't just want a mother for his son, who didn't want to live life safe. He was a man who wanted to take chances. He would not let her be a dragonfly who stayed out of reach.

He'd have to do his best to make her surrender.

"Guess who was looking for you in the VIP lounge last night," Kelli said the next day at the model fittings.

"I know," Rebecca said with little interest.

Kelli frowned as if annoyed that her fun and games had been ruined. "You don't seem to care."

"Because I don't."

"That's what I told him. I said you wouldn't give him the time of day."

"Why did you say that?"

"Because it's true, and he's no good for you."

Rebecca started to grin. "Because he didn't fall for your charms?"

Kelli looked at her closely. "I really think you should give up the idea of hosting your show here."

"Why would I do that?"

Kelli looked around, then lowered her voice. "Because I heard some workers talking about a curse."

Rebecca sent her a sharp look. "I don't believe that, and neither should you."

"I don't. I'm just not sure Aaron is a man who can be trusted to protect you."

"I don't need him to protect me. Hopefully, nothing else will go wrong."

"But if something else were to happen, would you cancel the show?"

"Nothing else will happen."

"But if it did," Kelli pressed.

Rebecca held up her hands. "I'm not having this conversation." She walked away to observe some of the volunteers helping the models, then looked at the rack of unopened garment bags.

She'd hardly slept last night after the kiss. Work was the only way to keep her from daydreaming about him. Rebecca wanted to know how it would feel to wake up in his bed, in his arms. To not just feel the touch of his lips on her mouth, but everywhere. She had to forget him. She'd love him from afar, but promised herself she would never get too close again.

"Did you sleep as little as I did last night?" came the whisper of a deep rich voice in her ear.

She froze at the sound of his voice. She should have expected he would find her, but she still hadn't planned on how she'd respond. She had to be distant but professional. She slowly turned to him and plastered on a polite smile. "Good morning."

"No, it's not. I—"

She held up her hand. "There's really nothing to say. I have a lot to prepare for, and I'd really appreciate if you didn't get in my way."

"You can try to ignore me, but you can't ignore what's happening between us."

"Nothing is happening," she said, then turned and unzipped a garment bag.

"You lied to me last night."

She looked at him, surprised. "What do you mean?"

"You said that I scared you, but if that were true, why aren't you scared of me right now?"

"Because there are people around us."

He shook his head. "No, that's the one thing I remember about you. You weren't afraid of me, or of spending the night in the Wethers mansion."

"I was different back then," Rebecca said, returning to the bag.

"I won't push you, but this isn't over," he said, walking away. "Not many things frighten you, Rebecca."

She stiffened when she saw something move. "Aaron?"

"Yes?"

"I am not afraid of you, but I am afraid of snakes."

"Snakes?"

"Yes, like this one," she said, staring at a multi-colored reptile that had slipped out of the garment bag. It lifted its head, as if posed to strike.

Chapter 8

"Stay quiet and still," Aaron said in a calm voice. The snake was one of the most poisonous on the island, and he didn't want it agitated. "Nobody move," he said, walking slowly toward Rebecca.

He grabbed a pair of scissors from a side table then flung them, hitting the snake in the head and killing it instantly.

Aaron rushed to her side. "Did it get you?" he asked, checking Rebecca's face and neck.

"No," she breathed, clinging to him because her legs felt weak. She briefly closed her eyes and rested her head against the safety of his chest. She wanted to fall apart, but knew she couldn't afford to.

"Are you sure?" he asked, lifting and checking her arm.

She pushed his hands away, both amused and embarrassed by his concern. "Of course I'm sure." She looked at the outfit stained with the snake's blood and guts. "Now it's ruined."

"You're making jokes now? Do you think this is funny?"

Rebecca looked up at him and lowered her voice, although she didn't let him go. "No, but I can't afford to fall apart right now. I am not going to give anyone an excuse to cancel my show, do you understand? Just let me hold on to you for another minute and I'll be fine."

He shook his head. "No—"

Sudden anger lit her eyes. "I watched a wretched disease take my mother way, I've seen my grandmother suffer the indignities of dementia, I've lived on two meals a day and I remember walking through an Ohio winter with the cold burning my skin because my boots were so old and worn, they offered little protection. When I say I'll be fine, I mean it. Don't ever question me."

"You need to stop jumping to conclusions and let a man finish. I was going to say 'nobody would doubt that.'"

"Oh."

"But you're itching to fight me, aren't you?" he said in a hard tone while his eyes swept over her face like a soft caress.

Rebecca licked her lips, knowing she should look away, that she should let him go, but she was unable to move. "I didn't come back here for that."

"What did you come back for?"

As she stared into his eyes, Rebecca realized that she couldn't pretend anymore, that she didn't want to. That this man had saved her life not once, but three times, and by doing so had earned the right of her heart, no matter how painful it was for her to admit it. *I came to see you,* she started to say before a well-dressed man, pressing a handkerchief to his face, interrupted her.

"Is she all right?" he said to Aaron. "We need to report this to security,"

"I'm sure it was nothing," Rebecca said, releasing her grip on Aaron's arm, but it was when she did so that she realized he'd also been holding on to her. His arm still braced her back. "Someone was probably careless when transporting the clothes," she said, trying to keep her voice steady. "It's really small and could have easily slipped in by itself."

"I'll join you in a minute," Aaron said to the other man. He wisely took the hint and left them alone. "I know you have a lot to do, but I need you to do one thing for me."

"What?"

"I need you to trust me."

"I already do."

"Good. I want you to keep up the charade that you're not scared until we have a chance to talk," he said, then let her go and walked away.

"He is scary," Kelli said as two people from security bagged the snake and took pictures. "Did you see what he did with the pair of scissors?" She imitated Aaron's swift throw. "Just one inch in the wrong direction, and he could have missed the snake."

"But he didn't," Rebecca said, putting her things away. *He saved my life and stole my heart.* She kept seeing flashbacks of Aaron and how he had taken a harmless pair of scissors and turned them into a lethal weapon. The cold look of his gaze still sent shivers through her, but the feel of his embrace made her skin burn.

"I wonder where he learned to do that. It's a shame it didn't help. You'll still have to cancel the show."

"Why?"

"Rebecca, don't you think things are getting a bit too dangerous around here?"

"I told you never to mention canceling again. Why are you so eager to keep mentioning it?"

"I'm nervous."

"Then feel free to leave. I can find someone else to help me."

"You know it's dangerous to take warnings so lightly."

"Warnings?" Rebecca said, surprised by the word.

"Yes, sometimes when things go wrong, it's for a reason."

"You don't think it was an accident?" Harvey said as he and Aaron inspected the garment bag.

Aaron's jaw twitched. "I'm beginning to hate that word."

"Sorry, sir."

Aaron had spoken with security, then instructed them to ban Rebecca from entering the exhibit hall until further notice. There had been some minor protest, but when he threatened to cancel the show, she relented. After knowing she was in safe hands, he'd called Harvey to help him look over the space and examine the snake. He didn't want to get the local police involved because then news would spread all over the island, and he wanted to avoid that. Harvey had spoken to the workers, and they hadn't seen anything out of the ordinary.

"Something is going on. Trident being in her villa is the only thing that doesn't make sense, but this snake incident changes everything."

"How did Trident get in her room? Maybe that's the key, because it's out of context with the other troubles."

"I don't know, but I think it was a test or a distraction. Or possibly a message. The perpetrator started with something big and harmless, then moved to something small and lethal. It's someone from the island. Most people don't know about this particular snake and how to handle it," Aaron said.

"A prankster perhaps? Anybody could have opened that garment bag besides Ms. Cromwell."

"No, Rebecca likes to inspect all her clothes, so she always opens the bags first."

"But she doesn't know anyone on the island," H.C. said, still looking confused.

"I'll ask her some more questions tonight, but first I need you to ask around discreetly."

"I will. What are you going to do?"

"I'm going to make some major changes. Some that Ms. Cromwell won't like."

Harvey started to grin. "But you won't give her a choice, right?"

"Exactly."

He had to get to her first and find out what she was doing, Harvey thought as he made his way to Rebecca's villa. But then he saw her in one of her disguises walking toward a taxi. He raced up to her and grabbed her hand. "Where are you going?"

"Into town."

"Why?"

"I can't tell you that."

"Why are you doing this to me?"

"What?"

"I know I may not be as magnetic as Wethers, but I'm still a man. I haven't told anyone what I saw. I've kept it buried here." He pounded his chest with his fist. "But every time I see you, after nearly getting hurt, you're in his arms. You have to tell me what's going on so that I can help you. I can't let you ruin the Red Beacon name or get yourself killed."

"I don't know what you're talking about. Please, no one can see us talking together."

"You think Wethers would get jealous seeing you with me?"

She shook her head. "No, that's not—"

"Are you playing us against each other? Is that your game?"

"H.C.—"

He released her and turned. "I am not as powerless as you think, and toying with me is a mistake."

"I'm not toying with you."

"Then tell me what you're up to."

"I can't. Not yet. I'm not who you think I am."

"What?"

"Please, I have to go," she said, then dashed into the taxi.

Harvey watched her go, then took out his phone and called Wethers. He wouldn't tell him the full truth yet of what he saw or suspected, but if she wouldn't save herself, he'd have to do it for her.

"What is it, H.C.?" Wethers asked when he picked up the phone.

Harvey sighed with a heavy heart, then said, "When you get a chance, you'd better ask Ms. Cromwell if she's hiding anything."

"You don't think she's been truthful with us?"

"I'm not sure."

Wethers was quiet for a long moment, then said, "Tell me what you know."

Things were getting too complicated. The other man had given her a strange look when she'd returned from walking on the beach to clear her thoughts, and she had only four days left. At this rate, there was a good chance that she'd have to cancel her show.

Rebecca walked along the path between the villas, trying to strategize her next steps. An ink-black night hung overhead while tiki lanterns lit her path. But she barely noticed them. She had to figure out what was happening. She didn't believe in curses, but someone definitely wanted to ruin her show.

"Is there something you should tell me?" came a dark voice from under the shadow of a palm frond.

Rebecca stopped and swallowed, recognizing the voice. "No."

Aaron emerged from the shadows, then held up his hands. "Relax, I just want to talk to you."

Rebecca folded her arms and took a step back. "Okay."

"Do you have any enemies?"

"I don't think so."

"Are you sure?"

"Yes, why?"

"You know why," he said.

She let her arms fall to her sides. "I don't know why someone is trying to scare me. Few people know about my fear of snakes. I know it was probably harmless—"

"No, it wasn't. That's what bothers me most."

Rebecca widened her eyes. "You think someone tried to kill me?"

"That's why I'm going to ask you again, do you have any enemies? You can lie to yourself, but don't lie to me. This was no accident. Someone doesn't want this show to happen."

"I don't know why." She touched her forehead, stunned. "Really, I don't." She started to walk past him. "But I can't think about this right now."

He shook his head. "You don't have to pretend anymore."

"What?"

He grabbed her hand, forcing her to stop. "You don't have to pretend that you're not frightened. I want you to trust me. You're safe now."

You're safe now. With those words, Rebecca felt the past and present colliding in her mind. He'd said those very same words to her after he'd saved her from drowning. The tears of a remembered pain gathered in her eyes. "Why does it always have to be you?" She wiped away a tear. "Why do you always have to see me at my worst? To see me at my most vulnerable? To see me so weak?"

"I don't see you as weak."

She looked down at where he grasped her hand. "You can feel me trembling, can't you?"

"Yes, that's why I need you to be honest with me. Have you noticed anything or anyone?"

"No."

"Is there something that's made you uneasy?"

"Yes."

"What?"

"You."

He released her hand, and that same look of pain crossed his face before he masked it behind a neutral expression. "I'm trying to help you."

"I know. That's the worst part. I don't want to need your help. Not again. Not like this. You scare me more than anything. Being with you terrifies me because every time I look at you, I see the disgust on your face when I told you I loved you."

Aaron glanced up at the dark sky, his shoulders dropping as if a load had been lifted from them. "I'm sorry. I didn't know you meant it."

"What?"

His gaze fell to her face. "I thought you were laughing at me."

"Why would I laugh at you?"

"Because everyone was at the time." He shook his head. "It's a long story."

"I'm patient."

He sighed and hung his head. "I'm embarrassed. Even after all these years, it's still a soft spot."

"Tell me anyway."

He looked at his watch. "I'll tell you after we've moved your things."

"Moved my things? Why?"

"Because you're staying at my place. Until you leave this island, I'm going to make sure that you're safe. You're never leaving my side."

Chapter 9

It was strange to be back. Rebecca walked into the mansion with new eyes. It was still grand and exquisite, but unlike in the past, it seemed tinged with a lonely sadness. She walked into the living room with questions swirling in her mind. What did he mean he didn't know she'd meant it? What was so embarrassing that he couldn't tell her? And who hated her enough to put a dangerous snake in one of her garment bags? She walked over to the far wall and no longer saw Aaron's diorama display on a side worktable. Instead, she saw books and statues lining the bookshelves.

"You've brought trouble with you." The words came from a soft voice behind her.

Rebecca spun around, startled by the unexpected voice, and saw an older woman, with a shock of white hair and eyes like clear black glass, sitting in a large chair. "I'm sorry, I didn't see you. I'm—"

"I know who you are." She lifted a long finger. "And you have dark branches surrounding you. You've brought trouble with you, and if you're not careful, someone will get hurt."

"If you don't want me to stay, I won't," Rebecca said. "I understand you not wanting a stranger in your house."

The older woman slowly rose to her feet. "You were here before."

"Yes, but I don't believe we met. I—"

The woman held up her hand. "No, don't tell me. I want to figure it out for myself." She walked around Rebecca, looking her up and down as she did so. "You returned for love, but destruction has followed you."

"I don't believe in curses."

The older woman smiled. "I didn't say you were cursed. Open your eyes, and you'll find the answer. It's closely tied to you."

The sound of excited footsteps pounding down the hallway stopped her reply.

"Is it true you're staying here?" Brandon asked, appearing in the entryway.

"Yes, for a few days," Rebecca said, then turned back to the woman. She was gone. Rebecca spun around in a full circle, amazed. "Where did she go?"

"Who?"

"The woman who was here. I was just talking to her."

"I didn't see anyone. Did my dad kill a snake?"

"Yes," Rebecca said, trying to orient her thoughts. She knew she hadn't imagined the woman.

"With a machete?"

"No, with a pair of scissors. He grabbed them like

this and then threw them," she said, imitating the motion.

"Wow...I wish I'd seen that. I'll have to ask him to show me. The Green Rama snake is one of the deadliest on the island."

"Yes," Aaron said, coming into the room. "And it's best to leave them alone."

"But you killed one today."

"How did you hear about that?" He held up his hand. "Never mind. It was foolish of me to think it would be kept a secret."

"Dad, Ms. Rebecca was telling me how you killed the snake like this," he said, throwing an imaginary pair of scissors. "Can you show me—"

"Another time. I have to talk to Ms. Rebecca in private."

"Okay," Brandon said, then left, pretending he was brandishing a machete and making his way through the jungle.

Aaron sat down and powered up his tablet. "I need to know your schedule for the remainder of your stay here."

"Does an old woman live with you?"

"What?"

"When I first came in here, I saw a woman sitting in that chair," she said, pointing to the now empty seat. "Then she stood up and walked around me and started saying strange things."

"Like what?"

"That I'd brought trouble with me."

Aaron rubbed his chin. "That's not much of a stretch, considering all the troubles you've had. She's usually right about things like that."

"Who is she?"

"You mean, what is she?"

Rebecca's mouth dropped open. "Is she a ghost?"

Aaron laughed. "No, she's a seer. She tends to see things in the fourth realm that we don't. She's also my grandmother. After my grandfather died, I had her come stay with me."

"Oh."

"Now, let's look over your schedule," Aaron said, returning his attention to his tablet.

"I don't need you as my bodyguard."

"Yes, you do." He patted the seat beside him. "Let's not fight about this. Sit down."

Rebecca sat across from him so that it would be easier to study him and not be affected by his nearness. "Tomorrow we'll do a rehearsal."

He typed the information into his tablet.

"Why shouldn't I have said I loved you?" she asked.

He froze.

"Did you hear what I said?"

He nodded.

"Tell me why."

He was quiet for so long that she wasn't sure he'd answer her. When he finally spoke, he kept his gaze lowered. "A few weeks before we met, I'd made an idiot of myself by announcing my love to a woman I'd hoped to marry, and wondered why she'd never said she loved me."

"What's wrong with that?"

"When I say 'announced,' I mean half the island heard it because we were in the radio studio where she worked, and live on the air."

"Oh, no."

"For weeks afterward, people kept shouting 'I love you' at me."

Rebecca covered her face and groaned. "No wonder you were so angry at me."

"But I shouldn't have spoken to you the way I did. I usually just walked away, but that night I lost it." He lifted his gaze to hers. "You have that effect on me." He set his tablet aside and walked over to her. He held out his hand. "Did you really mean it?"

Rebecca looked at his outstretched hand, then gave him hers. "Mean what?"

He clasped her hand and lifted her to her feet, drawing her close, his eyes never leaving her face. "What you said on the beach the other evening?"

Her heart jolted at the dark, sensuous tone of his voice. "What did I say?"

"Tell me I don't scare you."

"But you do scare me," she said, then cupped his face in her hands. "In the most wonderful way," she whispered, then pressed her lips to his. She meant to draw away, but he didn't give her the chance, covering her mouth in delicious possession, forcing her to succumb. This was what she'd dreamed of all those years ago. She met his passion with ferocity of her own, letting her heart speak without words. She wrapped her arms around him, pressing her body close, delighting in his groan of pleasure.

He abruptly stepped back, and she looked at him in confusion and hurt, wondering if he was toying with her, until she heard footsteps, and Brandon appeared.

"Ms. Rebecca, do you want to see Trident's house?"

"I'd love to," Rebecca said, hoping her voice didn't sound too breathless. "But in a minute."

He glanced at his watch. "Starting now?"

"No, you can show her later."

"But—"

"I'll let you know after dinner. Now, let us get back to work."

Brandon released a dramatic sigh, then left.

Rebecca fell into her seat. "You have good ears."

Aaron sat across from her and lifted his tablet. "It comes with practice."

"Do you think he suspects anything?"

"Don't worry about him. Why are you sitting all the way over there?" He patted his lap. "Come and sit here."

"I won't be able to focus."

He stood up and walked over to her. "But I need the practice."

"Practice?"

He pulled her to her feet and wrapped his arms around her waist. "Yes, guarding your body."

"You don't need to guard it so close."

He let his hand slide down her thigh. "Let me be the judge of that."

"Anyone could walk in on us."

"Doesn't that make this more fun?"

"Not if it's Brandon."

Aaron paused. "You have a point. We can finish this after dinner."

"I promised to see Trident's home after dinner."

"That's okay. Brandon has a bedtime." He winked. "I don't."

Chapter 10

"So you're still here," Aaron's grandmother said, taking a seat.

"Yes," Aaron said. "You weren't able to scare her off."

"I wasn't trying to scare her. I was just telling her the facts."

Brandon widened his eyes. "Did Nan tell you your future?"

"How many times must I tell you that I can't see the future? I just see the present in a different realm."

Brandon covered the side of his mouth with his hand and whispered, "She does. I heard her one time tell—"

"Eat your dinner," Aaron said. "It's bad manners to spill other people's business at the dinner table."

"How come you ran away when I waved at you?" Brandon asked, looking at Rebecca.

"I'm sorry?" she said, surprised by his question.

"The other day you were in town and I was on my school bus and waved at you and you ran."

"I wasn't in town."

"Yes, you were. I saw you."

"If she said she wasn't there, then she wasn't," Aaron said.

"But—"

"Probably a tourist who looked like her."

"But I know it was you. You looked a little scared."

Rebecca shook her head. "I'm afraid it wasn't me. I rarely have time to go into town. And if it had been me, I wouldn't have run away from you. I'd never do that."

"It's okay to make a mistake," Aaron said. "They say everyone has a twin somewhere."

"Well, isn't this cozy," came a new female voice.

"Aunty Candace!" Brandon said.

"When did you get in?" Aaron asked. "Have you eaten?"

"Of course not, why do you think I'm here?" Candace said, taking a seat. "Hi, Aaron, Rebecca. I hope the show is ready to go."

Aaron motioned to the maid, who immediately went into the kitchen to get another plate and utensils. "Almost."

"Dad killed a snake," Brandon said.

"Why did you have to kill a snake?"

"It was in one of the garment bags."

"You mean I left you in charge and things have gotten worse?"

"I'm looking into it. That's why Rebecca is here."

"Just like old times," Candace said with a significant look.

But it wasn't like that, Rebecca thought. So much had changed. Aaron had gotten married and divorced and had a son.

After dinner, Rebecca enjoyed listening to Brandon telling her about his school as he showed her where Trident lived. He took her to the back of the mansion and walked over to an area where a large cage jutted out of a wooden shed. It was enormous.

"They have to have a big cage so they can climb up high," he said eagerly, opening the door to the cage and inviting her inside. "See that large branch over there? He loves to go to the top and jump off." Rebecca was impressed with all that she saw, but kept frozen in place. She didn't want Brandon to know that she was just a little, tiny bit afraid of being in a cage with a wild reptile.

"I didn't know taking care of an iguana took so much work," she said.

Next, Brandon showed her the large heater under the cage, where Trident could go for basking if he needed to. "I have to make sure I check the temperature so that inside the cage doesn't get too hot or too cold. That's why he can go inside the wooden shed, if the cage gets too hot for him. And over here—this is where he has the most fun." Rebecca followed Brandon and saw a large, hand-painted plastic swimming pool. "This is Trident's own personal bathtub. At least once a week I fill it up and make sure he gets a nice soaking. I have to empty the water after his bath so that he doesn't drink it. I have to make sure he gets a fresh, large bowl of drinking water every day." Brandon spent the next forty-five minutes telling Rebecca all about what he fed Trident and how he liked to talk to him about what was going on at school. Trident was tame enough to come and sit on Brandon's shoulder and let him pet him while she was there. When Trident slithered off Brandon's leg and went to hide under a rock nearby, Rebecca suggested they go back to the house.

"You should come back in the fall," he said. "You'll really like it then. We have our festival, and it's so much fun. It's called the Feast of the Saints, and that's when we have a big parade and people dress up in colorful costumes. All over the island there are lots of fun things to do, but the biggest parade is in the main city, Maureux. It's named after one of the founding fathers of the island. He was the great-grandson of the famous pirate and helped the ingigi—"

"Indigenous," Rebecca supplied.

"Yes, indigenous people, get their rights and develop the island to what it is today. My dad says we're dependents."

"You mean descendants."

He nodded.

Later, as she opened the door to her room, she was still smiling, remembering—but the moment she walked in, she knew she wasn't alone. The moon seeped through the blinds and reflected on a pair of ink-black shoes in the corner. Rebecca turned on the lights and saw Aaron sitting in the plush chair—still and waiting. For a moment she didn't know whether to stay or run. Fear gripped her, but she wasn't sure why so she kept herself rooted in place. She felt his elemental power and strength from across the room.

His unbuttoned shirt showed his muscled chest, but it wasn't a vain display. The room was warm. Looking at him again reminded her of how much things had changed, and of how little she knew him. Not the man of her dreams, but the flesh and blood man whose golden-brown gaze could be as hard as steel or hot as fire.

"What are you doing?" she asked, trying to project a calm she didn't feel.

"Keeping an eye on you," he said. For some reason, in the stillness of the room his voice sounded darker and deeper. "I told you I wasn't leaving you alone."

"Do you plan to sit there all night?"

"No."

"Then what do you plan to do?"

"I expect an invitation."

"You're going somewhere?"

"Yes." He nodded to the bed. "Right there."

Rebecca grinned. "And what if the invitation doesn't come?"

He slowly rose to his feet. It was a casual, controlled motion that could have been frightening considering his size, but all she could think of was the soft touch of his lips and the feel of his arms around her. They both knew what would happen tonight, no matter how she teased him. "I'll have to be persuasive," he said, crossing the room and closing the distance between them.

"Like a gentleman?"

He shook his head. "No," he said, his heated gaze keeping her still, his voice sounding like silken oak. "When it comes to you, I feel like being anything but a gentleman." He traced a slow, seductive trail along her jawline with his finger. "First, I need you to solve a mystery for me."

She looked up at him, startled, feeling the mood change. "A mystery? I told you I don't know who—"

He pressed his finger against her lips. "Let me finish. Can you do that?"

She nodded.

"I've been trying to figure out one thing. When you ran out of your villa after finding Trident under your bed, were you naked under your robe?"

Rebecca grinned. "That's not much of a mystery. I'm sure you can guess."

"I don't like to guess," he said, loosening one button on her blouse. "I like to know."

"You could use your imagination."

"I already have. That doesn't satisfy me."

"Would you like me to replay the scene?"

"Replay?"

"Yes, so that you can get a full picture of all the events."

He frowned. "Couldn't you just tell me?"

"Yes, but I think this will be a lot more fun. First, I came in after a long day and started to undress," she said, removing her blouse and skirt.

Aaron sat on the bed. "You can slow this part down. I'd like to get the full gist."

"Well…before I took off my bra and panties, I grabbed my robe." She reached for her robe hanging on the back of the door.

His face fell. "Oh."

"Then I went into the bathroom and turned on the shower," she said, walking into the bathroom.

"Then you took off your bra and panties," he said, following her.

"No, then I put on a shower cap." She put it on. "And checked the soap and hung up my robe, and then took off the rest," she said, unclasping her bra.

"Wait, that was too fast."

"You can't unclasp a bra slowly."

"I'll show you how next time. Proceed."

She shimmied out of her panties. "Better?"

Aaron watched her, caressing her body with his gaze. "Beautiful... I mean, much."

"Then I got in the shower."

He quickly undressed, then joined her. "I need to follow this story closely."

"Of course."

He squeezed soap gel on a loofah. "Where did you start first?"

"With my arms," she said, reaching for the sponge.

He moved it out of reach. "Just tell me where and I'll do it for you. I want you to concentrate on the details of your story," he said, sliding the sponge down her back to the swell of her bottom.

"I didn't do that."

"You need to allow for some poetic license."

"Not too much license, or we may never leave the shower."

"Don't tempt me."

But she didn't have to. He made sure that every last inch of her body got his full attention, and then allowed her the same pleasure before they rinsed off and toweled each other dry.

"And then I put on my robe," Rebecca said, tying the belt. "Mystery solved."

"There's something else I want to know."

"What?"

"When will I get my invitation?"

Rebecca sauntered over to the bed, then lay on her side and loosened her belt. "I'm not sure I should."

"Why not?"

She swung the belt around in a lazy circular motion. "I don't usually sleep with pirates. You're not to be trusted."

"It's better to have me in bed with you."

"Why?"

"Because if I'm holding you, I can't be stealing anything else."

"Unless it's my heart."

"I'm not that kind of pirate." He climbed onto the bed and kissed her.

"A gentleman waits for an invitation. I haven't given you one yet."

"I told you, I'm not a gentleman, and I don't like to wait." He covered her mouth again.

"But you are a man of honor and duty who will fight until you can claim your prize."

His eyes darkened with emotion. "I'm already claiming it."

And he made her feel like a treasure chest filled with riches. His lips made her warm, his tongue made her wet, his hands made her wild. He caressed her breasts as if they were crystal goblets, her lips rubies. He slid his hands down her thighs as if they were a string of pearls. She arched into him, demanding more, and he obliged.

Her feelings for him had always been stronger than his. She knew it was unfair to ask for more, even though she wanted it. She wanted him to ask her to stay. She wanted to know that he truly desired her, not as something he had to protect, but as something truly important. When she no longer needed him, would his feelings wane? When the show was over, would they be over, too? She tried not to think of that. It felt too good to be with him. Her body cried out for him to love her as a woman. A whole woman, with her weaknesses and strengths.

She briefly wondered about his ex-wife. What had convinced him to marry her? She pushed away the pain of knowing that he'd loved and offered his life and possessions to someone else, while she didn't know what she was to him. Was she just a passing fancy? But he wiped her worries away with his passionate lovemaking, stirring up a divine ecstasy within her. This moment was hers. She may not be able to steal his heart, but tonight his body was hers.

Rebecca wrapped her arms and legs around him, staking her own claim, taking her own possession. "You are the true prize," she whispered. "And I won't let you go."

He laughed. "You'll grow weary of trying to hold on," he said with an edge of grim certainty. "But let's not talk about the future."

"No, there's no need to talk at all."

Chapter 11

He'd become a man obsessed. He didn't care about how Wethers had teased him about his new clothes and haircut. He wanted to look his best. Harvey sat in the bar lounge trying not to think about Rebecca, but failing. He couldn't seem to stop himself from loving her, wanting to be with her, though he knew that was impossible. Fortunately, being the carrier of her secrets made him feel special. He knew secrets could be dangerous things, but he was hungry for them, hungry for any chance to be close to her or by her side. To be of service. He sipped his drink, remembering the last time he saw her in town. She was in disguise again, wearing a floppy hat, glasses and shapeless clothes, but her beauty could not be hidden.

He found her at one of the stalls in the bustling marketplace that smelled of spicy beef, filled with the sound of people bartering in their native Creole around her. He wondered how she'd managed to get away from Aaron, impressed she'd been able to.

"What are you looking for?" he asked her.

She spun around, her eyes wide. "I'm beginning to think you're following me."

"No, I come here often. You can ask anyone." He looked around. "Where's Wethers?"

"Who?"

"Aaron. I know he's determined to stay by your side. He's not someone you can easily slip away from."

She looked nervous. "The truth is—"

"It's okay," he said quickly, seeing the fear on her face. "I understand you wanting your space."

She bit her lip. "I'm doing something I probably shouldn't."

"Wethers—"

"Can't know yet," she said in a rush. "And neither can—" She shook her head. "It's a lot more complicated than I thought it would be. I'll tell you everything soon because I trust you. I just need you to do something for me."

"Anything."

Which was why he now sat alone in a bar watching Kelli Davis. The most Kelli did was dance and flirt, so there wasn't much to report. He didn't know why Rebecca wanted him to watch her assistant. Did he suspect her of something? He glanced at his watch. She'd asked for a half hour, and the time was almost up.

"Looking at your watch won't make sure someone will come any faster," the bartender said.

"I'm not waiting for anyone."

The bartender looked unconvinced. "It's not like you to dress this sharp hanging around here, H.C."

"I'm trying something new."

"If she doesn't show, it's her loss."

Harvey grinned. "Thanks."

"If you're really looking, I have a cousin—"

"I'll keep her in mind," he said when his phone buzzed. Harvey glanced at it and saw a text from Rebecca, giving him a location to meet her. He left the bar with his heart racing, although he scolded himself to remain cool. He met her in a shaded enclave by the cove, where no one could see them. She rushed up to him, her face beaming. "H.C., I don't know how to thank you."

"I haven't really done anything."

"You've done a lot. Because of you I think I'm getting close to discovering the truth. Look at this." She held out a bag.

Harvey looked inside and saw an assortment of items that didn't make sense. "What is this?"

"Evidence. I think Kelli is behind the sabotage. I'm not sure why yet, but I'm getting some idea."

He looked up sharply. "How did you get these?"

"I went into her room. That's why I had you watch her."

He snatched the bag from her. "You can't do that. No one can use these as evidence if they were stolen."

"But I thought—"

"You weren't thinking."

"I found a small carrier that could hold a snake, and a disguise. I found that after the panel collapsed."

"We have to put these back and let the authorities find them."

"I can't go back there. Do you know the risk I took?"

"Then I'll do it, but don't do anything more." He'd find a way to resolve this once he replaced the items, then he'd tell Wethers.

Rebecca had never been much of a morning person and was even less so after the night she'd spent with Aaron. He lay sound asleep beside her, and she was about to snuggle closer when her cell phone rang.

She silently swore, snatched it off the side table and answered before it woke him. "Just a minute," she whispered, glancing at Aaron once more before she grabbed her robe and tiptoed into the bathroom, carefully closing the door. "Sorry about that."

"How's my darling?" her grandmother said.

Rebecca smiled. She loved when her grandmother was mentally lucid enough to talk. Those times seemed to grow shorter. "I'm fine, Gran."

"How was your show?"

"It's not for another three days, but it's coming along great," she said, not wanting to worry her.

"How is your sister?"

Rebecca sat on the edge of the tub. "The last time I spoke to her, she sounded fine."

"But how did she look?"

Rebecca paused. "I wouldn't know that, Gran, I haven't seen her."

"Why not? Isn't she staying with you?"

Rebecca sighed, saddened that her grandmother was already confused. She usually got more disoriented toward the evening. "No, she stayed behind to be with you."

"But she's not here."

"I'm sure she'll be back later," she said in a reassuring tone.

"Something's wrong," Gran said, sounding more urgent. "You should have seen her. You should have seen her."

"Gran, is a nurse with you?"

"She may be in trouble."

"Gran, it's okay. Let me talk to the nurse."

But her grandmother wouldn't listen. "My baby's in trouble. You must get help."

"Oh, wait," Rebecca said quickly. "Here she is. Rachelle just walked in."

Her grandmother paused. "She's there with you?"

"Yes, she's waving at me and making a face because she knew I didn't expect her."

"Let me speak to her."

"She really—"

"I have to hear her voice."

Rebecca sighed. "Okay, one minute." Rebecca took a deep breath, then affected her sister's voice, which wasn't hard, since it was identical to hers. "Becca's told me you've been worrying again."

"I can't help myself. Did you tell her about my dream?"

"Of course," Rebecca lied, knowing her sister had more of a tolerance to listen to her grandmother's crazy dreams than she did. "Now we have to go. Love you."

"Love you, too. Let me say goodbye to Rebecca."

"Okay." Rebecca waited a beat, then answered as herself. "It was great to hear from you."

"Let Rachelle help you."

"I will. Love you," she said, then disconnected and called the main desk of the nursing home where her grandmother was being cared for. It was located about twenty minutes from where her sister lived in Delaware. "Hello, I just spoke to my grandmother and she's in quite a state. Could you have someone go in and check on her?"

"Yes."

"And when my sister gets in, please tell her what happened."

"Your sister? Your sister hasn't been here for almost two weeks. Your uncle has been stopping by, so it's okay."

Rebecca hung up the phone, stunned. She paced the room. Her sister hadn't told her she'd been traveling when she last spoke to her. Could it be that those sounds of the tropical bird she'd heard in the background hadn't been from the TV? Could her sister be on the island, as well? Why? What was she up to?

Rebecca dialed her sister's number.

"Hello?" Rachelle answered after the first ring.

"I just spoke to Gran," Rebecca said, keeping her tone even.

"I'm glad. She loves hearing from you."

"And she asked me about you. She was worried."

Rachelle laughed. "She always worries about us. What's new?"

Her sister sounded so sincere, but Rebecca wouldn't

be fooled. Her sister could point to a blue sky and convince you it was green. "She got me worrying, too."

Rachelle's carefree tone shifted. "What do you mean?"

"Where are you? And don't lie to me. I know you haven't visited Gran in nearly two weeks."

"I call her every day."

"Where are you? Rachelle?" she asked when her sister fell silent.

"I'm in St. James."

"Why? Why haven't I seen you? Where are you staying? Why didn't you tell me?"

"Because I didn't want anyone to know. I thought it would be safer that way."

"Safer?"

"I followed you on a hunch."

"A hunch?"

"I felt that something might go wrong. I wanted to look out for you. The last time you visited this island, you came back so distraught—"

"You could have told me."

"And then things started to go wrong, and I started investigating things."

"Investigating?"

"Yes, and there's something you should know. Come and meet me, but don't tell anyone."

"I can't come until later this evening. My schedule is packed. Today I have a TV appearance and a radio interview, and I have to visit a local gallery."

"All work and no play," Rachelle said with a forced laugh.

"Tell me where you are and I'll—"

"I can't."

"Why not? You're alone, and I'm not. Besides, it will be difficult for me to get away from Aaron."

"Fine. Call me later so we can schedule a way to meet. It's important," Rachelle said, then disconnected.

Chapter 12

This was the last place he wanted to be, but he'd dine with the Devil if that would keep Rebecca safe. Having to see his ex-girlfriend Tonya again came close. Her career had risen in the ten years since their breakup. She had a voice for radio and a face for TV. Her syndicated TV show was a hit on both the island and abroad. He'd gotten over her, but the humiliation of his pathetic plea being broadcast live still lingered. He watched her getting her makeup touched up—not that she needed much; she was a natural beauty. She looked every bit like the smart, ambitious girl who'd escaped a broken home and become one of the most successful women on St. James. She had skin the color of rum, and light brown hair with blond highlights. She looked as sweet as treacle swimming in honey, but he knew better.

"Well, this is a surprise," Tonya said to his reflection in the mirror. She waved her makeup artist aside and swung her chair around to face him. "I never thought I'd ever see you here."

"Don't expect a repeat performance."

"People are curious about you. You would make a great guest."

Aaron shoved his hands in his pockets. "We know that will never happen. I'm here for one reason, and it's not you."

"Do you want to say anything about what's troubling the upcoming Cromwell Collection?"

"No, and if you dare mention it on air, I'll make you regret it."

A cool grin touched her lips. "Careful what you say." She pointed at him in a playful manner, her wedding ring catching the light. The stone was so large, Aaron was surprised she could raise her hand. He knew it was from her second husband.

"You can quote me on that. I know how you operate. I wouldn't be surprised if you were taping me right now."

"No, I don't do that anymore. So what's going on with you?"

"You don't really expect me to answer that."

"I can't help but be curious." She looked over at Rebecca. "She's a little like Ina."

"She's nothing like Ina."

"No need to get defensive. Maybe later we could—"

He shook his head. "Let's stop pretending we have anything more to say to each other. I just wanted to warn you."

"I have to do my job."

Aaron blinked. "And I'd hate to see it put in jeopardy," he said, then walked away.

Rebecca knew who Tonya was. She was the woman who had broken Aaron's heart, but meeting her in person was still a shock. She'd thought the woman who'd hurt Aaron would be a sly woman, not the smiley, button-nosed petite woman who greeted her. She put Rebecca at immediate ease, complimenting her designs and sharing her admiration for Rebecca's career before the cameras started taping. And Rebecca hoped for that same ease when they went live. For the first several minutes it was fine—that was, until Tonya went in for the kill.

"I've heard you've had a lot of problems with your upcoming show. Do you think your show is cursed?" she asked.

"That's an odd question," Rebecca said, determined to remain poised, even though the question caught her off guard.

"Is it? I've heard that your event has been plagued with several misfortunes so far."

"I know that we have a great team on board who are working to put together a stellar show." She shrugged. "If people are not interested in seeing a spectacular show and my latest collection, there's not much more I can say."

"But you *can* say something about the stage malfunction and the snake."

The little vixen was tenacious, but Rebecca was undeterred. She may not look as sweet, but she had a lot more will. "I don't believe there's anything to say.

I'd really hate to say anything against the wonderful people I've worked with here on St. James."

Tonya looked a little flustered by the response. Rebecca knew she'd put her on sticky ground, and she'd have to tread carefully. Rebecca stared at her, willing to let the silence lengthen, knowing that it was deadly on TV, but she wouldn't be provoked to up their ratings for anything.

"Tell us why you got into fashion," Tonya said in a desperate bid to save the interview.

Rebecca resisted smiling, although she knew she'd triumphed, and answered. From there the interview went exactly as *she* wanted it to. Once it ended, she took off her microphone.

Aaron approached her with a grim expression. "I don't know how she found out so much."

"Someone must have told her."

Aaron raised a brow, looking both pleased and impressed. "You handled her well."

"She looks as harmless as a cartoon bunny, but she's as lethal as a deadly spider," Rebecca said with a shiver.

"Fortunately, you didn't let her bite you."

"I wonder why she was so determined to talk about the mishaps," Rebecca said as they headed to the exit.

"Ratings. People like to hear bad news, especially when it happens to successful people."

"But she could tell right off that I wouldn't cooperate. She took a risk to try to press me."

Aaron abruptly stopped walking. "You're right. That's strange."

Rebecca looked at him, curious. "What is?"

"Tonya likes risk. She likes challenge and controversy."

"She didn't today."

"No, she didn't go as far as she usually does," he said, turning. "And I need to find out why."

"Do you want me to wait in the car?"

"No." He lifted his hand and motioned to one of the guards. When he came over to them, Aaron said something under his breath, then turned to Rebecca. "Stay with him, but stay within my sight. This won't take long."

When Tonya saw Aaron marching up to her, she held up her hands in surrender. "I was just doing my job."

"How did you know so much?" Aaron asked.

She let her hands fall and batted her eyes like a sweet child. "You know I can't reveal my sources."

Aaron folded his arms. "You could have pressed harder. Why didn't you?"

"I didn't have a choice."

"Of course you did. I've seen you make people cry."

"I know when I'm being baited. If I'd kept going, she would have made me seem as if I were bad-mouthing the island."

"The truth hurts. Viewers understand that."

"But I didn't want to risk my reputation on their understanding. I had her on the show and mentioned her troubles. That will have to be enough."

"Did you stop because of me?"

Tonya held up her hand, proudly flashing her ring. "I'm completely over you. You're the one who hasn't gotten over me."

"Yesterday, you may have been right about that."

Her smug expression faltered. "Yesterday?"

"Yes. Yesterday, I was still the man who hated the thought of how much he'd once loved you. A man who'd truly cared about you before all this. Who knew you when your nickname was 'Tacky Tonya' and you only had three shirts and two skirts."

"Don't ever say that name again."

"I never have, until just now. I knew how much it hurt you. Yesterday, I was still the man you'd so enraptured that he defied his family's disapproval to see you. Who still cared, even after your cruel prank humiliated him."

Tonya blinked back tears. "It was just a joke. But that was years ago. Why bring it up?"

"When did you stop being human? When did you stop using your pain and hurt as empathy and instead begin using it as a weapon? When did you just become a voice on the radio or a face on TV?"

Tonya's tears dried up. "Success has its price."

"Success?"

"Someone like you wouldn't understand that. I wanted to be with you, but I grew sick and tired of people thinking I'd gotten my radio show because of your connections. I hated how everyone seemed to give you credit for *my* success." She tapped her chest. "I wanted to prove that I was stronger, that you were the one who needed me."

Aaron smiled without humor. "Yes, that's the fire I expected to see. Who are you afraid of?"

"No one. I just think what's been happening there is odd."

Rebecca knew she had to tell Aaron about Rachelle, but she could never find the right time. After the TV show, she made an appearance at a local gallery, then gave an interview with a reporter. Twice she ducked into the ladies' room to call her sister, but only managed to reach her voice mail.

"Aaron, there is something I have to tell you," Rebecca said as they left the reporter's office. "Though it might be nothing."

"Okay," he said, then his cell phone rang and he looked at the number. "Just a minute. I have to take this."

Rebecca watched him listen, and then his face changed to an expression she'd never seen before and hoped to never see again. "I'll be right there," he said.

"What's wrong?" she asked, trying to keep up with his swift pace as they headed to his car.

"It's H.C."

"What about him?"

"He's been arrested."

Chapter 13

Aaron pinned Harvey with a hard look as they sat in the jail cell. "What has gotten into you? Changing your looks is one thing, but breaking into a guest's room? What were you doing in Kelli Davis's villa?"

Harvey sat opposite him with his head lowered, looking defeated. "I had my reasons," he said in a quiet voice.

"Tell me what's going on."

He shook his head, defiant. "I can't, not yet. Not until I get to speak to her."

"Who?"

He lifted his head. "Rebecca."

Aaron paused, then narrowed his eyes a fraction. "Why do you have to speak to her?"

"I'll explain later."

"You'll explain now."

Harvey looked up at the ceiling, then pointed. "Look, someone wrote their name. I wonder why they did that."

"Don't toy with me, H.C.," Aaron warned .

Harvey squinted at the writing. "It doesn't make sense. Why would someone want to be remembered in a place like this?"

The silence that followed his statement fell with such a potent weight that he was forced to look at Aaron.

"Start talking," Aaron finally said.

Harvey reached for his handkerchief, then realized he didn't have it and sighed, letting his hand fall to his lap. "No."

Aaron stared back at him for a few moments, not sure he'd heard correctly. H.C. never said no to him. "I'm sorry?"

"I said no."

"Why not?"

"I have to talk to Rebecca first."

"Why would you need to talk to her instead of me?"

Harvey waved his hand. "Not instead, just before," he clarified.

"This isn't like you. Don't be an idiot—"

Harvey rose to his feet in anger. "Do you really have so little respect for me? Do you think I'd be in this place for my own amusement? Don't you think I'd have a good reason? I've served you and your father before you, and I've never doubted you, even when I disagreed. Why? Because we both honor a code—a code of duty. What I need to say to Rebecca has nothing to do with you."

"Rebecca has everything to do with me."

"There are some things you don't know."

"You work for me. And your job—"

"I know my job," Harvey rudely interrupted.

"Tell me what you know."

"Let me speak to Rebecca."

Aaron took a menacing step toward him. "My job is to protect her."

"I know, and I have to protect her, too," Harvey said, standing his ground.

"From what?" Aaron demanded.

"From you."

Aaron stumbled back as if Harvey had struck him. "From me?"

"Yes. You don't know the power of your anger, and I don't want to expose her to that."

"Rebecca understands me."

"She's not as strong as you think. You could hurt her."

"I'd never do that," Aaron said, his voice raw.

"You wouldn't do it intentionally, but you're a hard man, Wethers."

"Did she tell you that I frightened her?" Aaron asked, suddenly unsure.

"No, but she doesn't have to. Where is she now? I bet you have her out in the waiting area with a guard you trust. Correct?"

Aaron nodded.

Harvey smiled, pleased that he'd been right. "See? I know you well. You're not the only man with honor and a desire to protect. I may not have your money or power, but I have my reasons for what I did, and that should be enough for you."

Aaron swore, then nodded. "Okay," he said, then left Harvey and found Rebecca in the waiting area just as Harvey had guessed. "He wants to talk to you."

"Me? Why?"

"I don't know," he said with frustration glittering in his gaze. "He's adamant about it." Aaron looked at Rebecca for a long moment, thinking of how H.C. felt the need to protect her from him. He never wanted her to be scared of him. He wanted to be the one— the only one—she turned to.

He drew her into his arms and kissed her, groaning deep when his tongue tasted the sweet flavor of her mouth. "Remember that," he whispered against her lips before he let her go.

Rebecca's lips still burned from Aaron's kiss, but she didn't have time to wonder about it because soon a guard led her to Harvey's cell. "I half expected you not to come because of Wethers," he said, pleased by the sight of her.

Rebecca sat down, feeling a little uneasy by the joy on his face. "You have to tell me everything that happened."

He frowned. "You know what happened. I was dumb enough to get caught."

"Did I ask you to go into her room?"

"You know you didn't. Rebecca, why are you acting this way?"

"So you think you saw me?"

"I *know* I saw you."

"What was I wearing?" she asked.

He scratched his head, annoyed. "Why are you asking me this?"

"Because it's important."

"You were wearing your regular disguise—a dress, floppy hat and glasses."

Rebecca leaned back and sighed. "I was afraid of that."

"Of what?" He leaned forward. "Rebecca, what's going on?"

"H.C....last night I was with Aaron."

His face fell. "Are you saying I'm imagining things?"

"No." She bit her lip. "I think you saw my sister."

He made a face. "Your sister?"

"Yes, my identical twin."

"You have a twin?"

Rebecca nodded. "Yes. She was born a few minutes before me, so we always joke that she's older. She also likes to look out for me. I just found out she's on the island, and I'm supposed to meet her to find out why."

"You mean it wasn't you in town or at the market last night?"

"No."

"Your sister," he repeated, looking relieved. "You have a wonderful, beautiful sister."

Rebecca couldn't help a smile. "I see she made an impression on you."

"What's her name?"

"Rachelle."

"What does she do? Where does she live? Where is she right now? What—"

"I don't know where she is right now," Rebecca said, holding off his questions with a wave of her hand. "She'll have to answer your other questions later, but first I have to get in touch with her and get her to help clean up this mess." She stood and turned.

"Maybe you shouldn't," Harvey said, standing, as well. "Wethers can get me out of here. Perhaps we shouldn't bring her into this."

Rebecca turned to him, confused. "Why not?"

"She kept her identity a secret for a reason. I was in Kelli's villa because we think she's the culprit, but we need to catch her the right and legal way to make sure the case sticks. We don't have a strong motive."

"Kelli?" Rebecca said in disbelief. "My assistant?"

"Yes."

"But she couldn't. She's—"

"We found some things in her place."

"Why would she want to stop the show?" Rebecca asked, refusing to believe his claim. "And the snake—"

"I don't think it was intentional. Many foreigners confuse the poisonous ones with the more harmless type. Maybe you did something to her in the past."

"No, Kelli's not like that. We always got on fine. I can't believe that Kelli would have anything to do with this. I won't believe it."

"Talk to Rachelle first, then get back to me."

"But how will Aaron get you out of here if—"

"Don't worry," Harvey said with a knowing grin. "Wethers and I know how to work the system. Just find your sister."

Rebecca left Harvey's cell, feeling as if she'd walked into her own prison. What a horrible reality if it were true. Could her assistant really be behind everything? Rebecca wondered about this as she slowly walked down the jail hallway. She remembered how upset Kelli had been when she'd told her she was staying with Aaron.

"What am I supposed to do?" Kelli had asked her as Rebecca packed.

"Everything you've been doing."

"But you don't need me as much if you have him following you everywhere."

"Kelli, I don't understand why this bothers you. You'll still get paid. I need you to help organize the volunteers. You're crucial to this show."

"Why won't you listen? You could get hurt next time."

"Aaron won't let that happen."

"How do you know?" Kelli challenged. "I thought you said you weren't interested in him."

"He saved my life twice." *Three times,* she wanted to say, but knew it was better not to. "I'll be okay, and you can enjoy some more freedom. Take this as a semi-holiday in that you don't have to follow me around anymore." But Kelli still looked concerned, and now Rebecca wondered why she had been so against her being with Aaron. Why had she been so insistent that she cancel the show? Why was she so worried that Rebecca could get hurt? No, Kelli couldn't be the culprit. Her concern had been real. It had to be someone else. Rebecca groaned. And now her sister was here. Should she tell Aaron? H.C. seemed to think she should, and he knew Aaron better than she did. They had met only a couple of days before the show.

Aaron found Rebecca as she exited the police station. "Well?" he asked.

"He suspects Kelli," Rebecca said as she went down the stairs.

"And he couldn't tell me that?"

"He wanted to tell me first."

"Why?"

It was a good question. Too bad she couldn't answer it fully. "I had some suspicions that he followed up on."

Aaron took her arm, stopping her. "Suspicions you didn't tell me about?"

"They seemed harmless, but H.C. took them more seriously than I expected." She rubbed her forehead. "I feel awful about this. I just need to go home and rest."

Aaron looked as if he wanted to say more, but something in her expression stopped him. He gently took her hand. "Come on, then."

Of course she didn't rest once she got back to the mansion, although she was able to convince Aaron to leave her alone. She waited a few moments before she called her sister. She got her voice mail. After three more tries, she just left a message. Rebecca checked the hallway to make sure it was clear. She didn't want Aaron asking questions, but needed to get out of the house.

She exited the back of the mansion and looked in Trident's enclosure. She grinned when she saw where Candace had put an ugly statue she'd shown her earlier. One of the models who had gotten sick had given it to her, and told her to keep it for her. But Candace, being Candace, didn't see any use for the object and decided to get rid of it. Rebecca stared at the creature, wishing it had some sort of magical powers to give her some answers. She looked closely and off to the side. Behind the cage, she saw a bit of white that she hadn't seen before. She reached down and found crumpled balls of paper. She smoothed them open and saw Brandon's math exams—they were filled with glaring red marks.

She went back inside and went up to Brandon's room, where he was playing a video game. "What's this?" she asked, showing him the papers.

His gaze darted left and right like a trapped animal looking for a way to escape. "Please don't tell my dad."

"He should know. Then he can help you."

"I don't want him to know I'm stupid."

"You're not stupid."

"I'm not as smart as my dad."

"I'm going to show you how wrong you are. Give me a piece of paper."

He did.

"Now, I need you to pretend to be like your dad, and you own your own resort," she said, writing numbers on the paper then tearing it in columns. "You have three villas that are empty, and they each cost three hundred dollars."

Brandon laughed. "Wow, that's a lot of money! You know I can count to a thousand."

"Are you ready to deal with thousands?"

He quickly shook his head. "No. Two hundred is fine."

"I said three hundred, pay attention. Now, if I gave you five hundred dollars for a room, what would my change be?" she asked, handing him the paper money she'd created.

He took the money, then set it down. "I don't know."

"You haven't tried."

"Why are we doing this anyway? The teacher always asks us about buses and coconuts."

"If you won't let me help you, I'll have to tell your father."

"Okay, okay," Brandon said, lifting up the paper money and studying it.

"Don't get frightened by the extra two zeros. Forget them. What's five minus three?"

"Two."

"And if you added two zeros after that two, what is it?"

"Two hundred," he said with new understanding.

"Good. Let's try counting money."

He made a face of disgust. "Money's hard."

"But it's important. Remember, you're pretending to be your dad."

He nodded. "My dad's really good with money."

"And you will be, too."

Rebecca spent the next half hour with Brandon. She knew there were other things she should be doing, but helping Brandon was a nice distraction. She remembered that growing up, she had a major math phobia, and it was a kind teacher who took the time to help her overcome her fear. Besides, most of the major details had been attended to, and the show was scheduled to go on as planned. Kelli had been left to take care of last-minute details, and nothing had gone wrong. So wasn't that proof she was innocent?

"That was fun!" Brandon said, feeling pleased with himself after completing several more exercises Rebecca made up.

"Now, let's see why this is wrong," she said, laying out his exam.

"You won't tell my dad about this, right?" he asked, looking anxious.

She felt guilty about keeping another secret from Aaron, but knew he had enough to worry about already. "If you fail your next exam, you promise me you'll tell him?"

"Yes. I wish you could stay."

She looked at him with affection. "I can always come back and visit."

"It's not the same," he said.

And Rebecca didn't know what to say, because she knew he was right. But would Aaron ever say what his son had the courage to?

"How's school?" Aaron asked his son at dinner that evening.

Brandon glanced at Rebecca as if afraid she'd reveal something. She kept her gaze fixed on her plate.

"Brandon?" his great-grandmother said.

He turned to her. "Yes, Nan?"

"Your father just asked you a question."

"School's good," he mumbled.

Aaron watched him closely. "You don't sound sure."

"I am."

"Good." Aaron cut his fish. "Did you rest well, Rebecca?" he asked. The question sounded casual, but she knew it was not.

"Yes."

"You didn't rest very long," he said, catching and holding her gaze.

"What do you mean?"

"I went in to check on you, and you weren't there."

"I couldn't sleep, so I went to look at Trident." At least that was true. She didn't need to tell him that she was anxious about H.C., worried about Kelli and frustrated that she hadn't been able to reach her sister. "I know this might sound strange, but being around nature helps calm me."

Aaron nodded, but she wasn't sure he completely believed her.

Later, she waited until Aaron left the room they shared and went to tuck Brandon in bed before she returned to the bedroom and tried her sister again. But she still just reached her voice mail. She gripped the phone, wondering what she should do next. Had something gone wrong?

"You're hiding something from me," Aaron said from behind her.

Rebecca spun around. She hadn't even heard him enter. He moved like a thief, and it was times like this that his ancestry was most apparent. "No, I—"

Aaron waved his finger, halting her words. The gesture looked more innocuous than it really was. "Who have you been trying to call all day?" he asked.

"Someone with the show," Rebecca said, keeping her tone casual. She set the phone down, pleased that her hands weren't shaking. "But that doesn't matter now." She turned and kissed him. Lying wouldn't work, but seduction may. And it would be much easier. "I have so much on my mind, and I feel so tense. How do you unwind?"

His voice deepened. "There are a number of ways."

She rested a hand on his chest. "Care to tell me how? Better yet. Show me."

"I have a Jacuzzi bathtub and a pool."

She unbuttoned his shirt. "I like it better when you make me wet."

"You think that will help you unwind?"

"I know it will," she said slowly, pushing his shirt from his shoulders. "You help me forget."

"And what do you want to forget?" he asked, his intense gaze searching her face.

Rebecca fought to keep her voice light under his focused scrutiny. He could never know her real reason. "Just the stress of the day," she said, letting her hands fall to his trousers.

Aaron covered her hand and stopped her so swiftly that she cried out in surprise. "I have rules I live by," he said in a velvet tone laced with steel. "I don't mind being used as a bodyguard, or used as a diversion, but I will not be used as a cover."

Rebecca blinked, surprised by the fierceness in his tone and his words. "What?"

"Sleep with me if you want to, not because you need to," he said, his bold gaze daring her to look or draw away from him. "I'm not stupid, Rebecca. I can tell when a woman wants to sleep with me because she has a hidden agenda. A man like me gets used to it. Used to seeing the power of my name or the wealth of my business shining in a woman's gaze, her greed honeying her words and perfuming her skin. Women like that make sure they smell sweet and say the right things, hoping that I won't notice that as they're wrapping their legs around me, they're checking their watch to see how long it will take."

"But I'm not after that."

His eyes flashed. "Then what are you after?"

"Nothing."

"I don't know what's worse. Knowing that you're lying, or not knowing what you truly want. That's what's worse—I can't figure out what you're after right now, but it's not me."

She grabbed his arm when he turned. "No, please, I don't want to be alone."

His jaw twitched with fury. "Don't lie to me."

"I'm not lying."

"Then stop pretending."

"I'm not pretending, either. Not about this. I do want to be with you. I want you to stay with me."

"Why? If I left, you can call whoever you've been trying to reach."

"Don't do this," she said in a soft plea. She didn't want to lose him. She didn't want him to walk out of the room, feeling that she'd used him or that she was hiding something, even though that was true. Their time together was too precious to her.

"What?"

"Make me break a promise."

"To H.C.? What are you two hiding from me?"

"*Promise* is the wrong word. We just have a puzzle piece that might or might not fit."

Aaron briefly squeezed his eyes shut and hung his head. "How am I supposed to protect you if you don't trust me?"

"I do, but—"

"But what?" he pressed, then released a heavy sigh. "Are you afraid I'll get angry? Did you tell H.C. that you were scared of me?"

"No."

He held her hand. "I may get angry and be impatient, but I'd never hurt you."

"I know that," she said, caressing the worry from his face. "Just give me a day to figure things out."

She didn't know whether it was her words or voice, but she saw something in his expression and stance change—soften—and she felt her fear loosen. "Fine, I won't ask you any more questions right now."

"And I wasn't playing games," she said, tugging on the waistband of his trousers in a teasing gesture. "I do want to unwind."

"You want to distract me," Aaron said in an indulgent tone.

"That, too," Rebecca said, unzipping his trousers, then pulling them down. "You seem as tense as I am. Is it wrong for me to worry about your well-being?"

"Not if you mean it," he said, removing the rest of his clothes.

"I do."

"How can you say you care about my well-being when you're driving me crazy?" he asked, then covered her mouth in a wild, hungry caress. He stripped off her clothes with speed, but control, claiming her body with precise mastery. "If it were anyone but you, I'd get the answers I seek," he said, kissing the moist hollow of her throat. He lifted her in his arms. "I'd make you uneasy."

"I already am."

"Not enough," he breathed, laying her on the bed,

then covering her with his body. "If you were anybody else, I wouldn't surrender so easily."

Rebecca looked down the length of his body,
feeling the heat of his hard chest pressed against her
breasts. "You call this surrender?"

A sensuous smile touched his lips. "Do you deny
your conquest?"

"I don't think anyone can conquer you."

"It won't work," he said, teasing her ear with his
tongue.

"What?" she asked, feeling her toes curl.

"Trying to tease me with your modesty," he whispered.

Rebecca laughed, running her fingers down the
length of his back. "I can hardly call this being mod-
est."

"You don't even realize the true power you have
over me, do you?" he said with feeling. "That's good.
I'll use it to my advantage."

"Right now you have all the advantage."

"And it's still not enough," he said, then kissed
her response from her lips, making her forget what
she was about to say—and everything else. He took
every opportunity to remind her of how much he ruled
her heart. When they were through, she lay still in
the safety of his embrace, ready to drift off to sleep.

Aaron rubbed his thumb over her taut nipple. When
he spoke, his warm breath tickled her skin. "Do you
know one of the reasons my marriage fell apart?"

Rebecca paused, no longer feeling at ease. "No."

"Lies and secrets. I abhor them."

She delicately cleared her throat. "I agree about
lies, but sometimes secrets have their place."

"Not in my house," he said softly.

"Not all secrets are bad."

His eyes clung to hers. "They can still erode trust."

"You don't trust me?"

"You won't tell me everything about your conversation with H.C., and now I even see you having private looks with my son."

"It's a surprise. Brandon wants to surprise you, and I said I'd help."

"What kind of surprise?"

"You'll find out later."

He lifted a brow. "I told you I hate to wait."

"You'll do it for him."

"What about H.C. and the person you keep calling?"

"Did you find out anything more about Kelli? Were you able to get H.C. released? He said you would—"

He pressed a finger over her mouth. "You first."

Rebecca sighed, tired of keeping secrets from him. He was right—secrets were eroding the tenuous bond between them. "I've been trying to reach my sister, and I haven't been able to."

"Why? Is there something wrong with your grandmother? I know you told me she looks after her."

"No, I found out that Rachelle is here on the island, and she's the reason H.C. broke into Kelli's place."

"That doesn't make sense."

"He thought she was me. We're identical twins."

Aaron looked at her with renewed interest. "I didn't know you were a twin."

"It's not something I share. I want her life as separate from mine as possible."

"I see."

"But she's been up to something on the island, and that's why H.C. got caught up in it. They think Kelli is the one creating havoc."

"With what proof?"

"He won't say. And I don't believe it, but he wants me to talk to Rachelle first."

Aaron kissed her on the forehead then leaned back. "You don't have to worry about your sister. She's safe."

Rebecca sat up and stared at him. "What? You knew?"

"Yes," he said, looking self-satisfied. "I wanted to see what you would tell me."

"But how did you know, and when did you—"

"This morning. I heard you answer the phone and listened while you were in the bathroom."

"Eavesdropping."

"I was doing my job," he corrected. "While you were at the TV station, I got your sister's number from your mobile and called her and told her not to speak to you."

"Why?"

"Because I wanted to see how much you trusted me. Not much, by the look of things."

"H.C. told me not to, and I wasn't sure—"

"You still should have told me. What if something had happened to her? This island isn't just a holiday paradise. It has a dark side, too."

"You're right," Rebecca admitted with reluctance. "I'm sorry. I won't keep something like that from you again."

"Hopefully there will never be another reason to."

"So even when we were at the jail, you knew?"

"I didn't know or suspect she was your twin until what happened to H.C., then I started to put things together. She'll be coming here to the house tomorrow. It's time all this comes out in the open."

"I agree. I just need one thing from you."

"What?"

"When she comes, let me talk to her first—alone."

Chapter 14

"Do you have any idea of how much trouble you've caused?" Rebecca asked her sister as they sat in Aaron's living room the next day.

"I was trying to help you," Rachelle said with a sigh.

"H.C. was arrested, the reputation of the resort was on the line because H.C.'s an employee, and—"

"I know, I know," she said, waving her hands in surrender. "I didn't mean for all this to happen."

"Why did you pretend to be me?"

"So that I could watch Kelli and gather some information in town."

"What made you think of her?"

"There was just something about her that worried me, and after doing a search I found a connection between her and this island."

"What?"

"She's been coming here every year for eight years. She stays at one of the hostels and keeps to herself. Obviously, she's never been able to afford staying at Red Beacon Villa Resorts, or maybe she has a reason to stay away."

"That's hardly criminal," Rebecca said.

"Why pretend to never have been here before?"

"I've never asked her. I'm sure she would have told me if I had."

"I just get the sense something bad happened. In town, she's been known to go to a local spiritualist."

"Again, that's not criminal. What brought you here in the first place?"

"Gran had a dream."

Rebecca rolled her eyes and slapped her forehead. "You didn't really fall for that."

"It proved to be true. Something is wrong with your show, or rather, was. Aren't you glad that I might have solved this?"

"You don't know Kelli like I do. There's no real proof."

"That's where Aaron can help us."

Harvey looked toward the hallway with concern. "Maybe we should go and see how they are," he said. He had been with Aaron in the sitting room for the past twenty minutes.

"No, give them more time," Aaron said, not looking the least bit concerned about what was going on.

"They could be fighting."

Aaron shrugged. "Or having a heated debate, or talking about the price of bread."

Harvey reached for his handkerchief, then stopped and drummed his fingers instead. "This isn't funny."

"No, and that's why I'm not going to intervene yet."

Harvey stood. "I—"

"Sit down. I promised Rebecca that I'd let her talk to her sister alone, and I intend to keep that promise."

Harvey sat down. "But how much time does she need?"

Aaron shrugged again. "Rebecca will let me know when she's ready." Aaron looked at Harvey with a grin. "And Rachelle will appreciate it, too."

"What?"

"Now I understand it all," he said, gesturing to Harvey's new shirt and haircut. "You like her, don't you?"

"It's not like that."

Aaron's grin widened. "I know you too well, H.C."

"Yes, I like her."

"We're lucky she wasn't Rebecca. Otherwise we'd both be in trouble. You looked ready to hurt me in jail."

Harvey couldn't help a grin. "I didn't know I had it in me."

"When are you going to make your move?"

"I'm sure she'll be leaving the island soon."

Aaron pointed at him. "Then convince her to stay."

"Are you going to do that?"

Aaron shook his head and rested his hand on the table. "My situation is different."

"How?"

"I have a son and a lot more baggage."

Harvey sniffed, unconvinced. "You're too afraid to ask her."

"I'm not afraid," Aaron said, too relaxed to be provoked by Harvey's words. "I'm just not interested right now."

"Then why even start anything?"

"Why not? I still like to enjoy myself."

"If you love Rebecca half as much as I love Rachelle, you're in trouble."

Aaron laughed. "Spoken like a true romantic. Something I'm not. Once you've been burned by love and marriage, you're a lot more cautious. I almost envy your untainted outlook. Cherish it."

"What are you two doing?" Candace asked, walking into the room. "Wow, looking sharp, H.C. When did this happen? I was only gone a week."

Aaron cast a glance at her. "Go into the kitchen if you're hungry. We already ate."

"What's going on?" Candace asked, taking a seat. "I'd hoped to talk to Rebecca about the announcer for the show."

Aaron stiffened. "What about the announcer?"

"He got himself drunk and in a bar fight. He has a black eye and several broken ribs, so we can't use him."

Aaron swore.

Harvey groaned. "Maybe the show is—"

Aaron shot him a glance. "Don't say it."

"We have to find someone quick," Candace said. "Someone with a great speaking voice who knows about the show."

Aaron glanced at Harvey. Candace did the same and smiled.

Harvey held up his hands, as if reading their minds. "Oh, no. Not me."

"Why not?" Candace said. "You should show off your new fashion sense."

"But—"

"Think of how happy Rachelle would be to hear what you're doing for her sister's show," Aaron said.

"Who's Rachelle?" Candace asked.

"Do you really think so?" Harvey asked with hope.

"She'll be very impressed," Aaron said. "If I were in your shoes, I'd use it as a great opportunity."

"Who is Rachelle?" Candace asked again.

Harvey nodded. "Okay, you've got yourself an announcer."

"Thank you."

Candace pounded the table with her fist, making both men jump. "Who is Rachelle?"

"Rebecca's sister," Aaron said. "We're waiting for her to finish talking to her right now."

"Her sister is on the island?"

"Twin sister," Harvey added.

Aaron waved his hand before his sister could ask. "It's a long story," he said, and before he could elaborate, Rebecca and Rachelle appeared in the entryway. "We're ready to talk now," Rebecca said.

Candace gaped at them, then stood up. "Amazing!"

"Are you sure you're identical?" Aaron said. "I just don't see it."

Everyone turned to him, surprised.

"What?" he said, perplexed by their looks. "Sure, I can see the resemblance, but they don't look exactly the same."

"Yes, they do," Candace said.

"But Rebecca's—" He stopped.

"Eyes aren't as brown," Harvey finished.

Aaron shot him a glance. "Of course they are."

Rachelle grinned at Aaron. "You think she's prettier, don't you?"

Aaron stood, looking uneasy about being put on the spot. "Never mind. I'm sorry I mentioned it. Let's go talk about what's really important," he said, then walked past them into the living room.

Rachelle looked at her sister. "You know what this means, don't you?"

Rebecca knew, but still couldn't believe it. Her grandmother always liked to tell them that there would be a man who would recognize and be able to tell them apart. She'd always considered it a silly family story, but now she wasn't so sure. "Let's go."

"Harvey's our new announcer," Candace said. "The other guy got in a fight, and H.C.'s saving us from a big headache."

"Oh, thank you, H.C.," Rebecca said, taking Harvey's hand and giving it a gentle squeeze.

Aaron popped his head back in the room. "What's taking you so long?"

"We're coming," Rebecca said. But before she followed him, she saw her sister give Harvey a quick kiss on the cheek. He smiled in return.

But minutes later they sat in the living room, all good humor and smiles gone.

"We have to get her to confess," Rachelle said after she'd shared all that she'd uncovered.

"How will we do that?" Harvey asked.

"I don't know."

"She can't create any more havoc," Aaron said. "I've been having her watched."

"I still don't believe it's her," Rebecca said. "We need to know the true motive."

"I think it's simple jealousy."

"Or maybe it's greed," H.C. said. "Maybe she thought she could convince Rebecca to sue Red Beacon Villa Resorts and wanted part of the money."

"She wanted me to cancel the show because she was worried about me," Rebecca said. "I know the snake incident scared her, too."

"There haven't been any other incidents since then, right?" Candace asked. "So it might be her or—"

"Plus, Wethers has been around," H.C. interrupted. "I'm sure he wasn't part of her plan."

"I don't know how you can be positive it's her," Rebecca said.

Rachelle threw up her arms. "What more do you need to convince you? You didn't know she was familiar with the island, she had a snake carrier in her room, she disappeared at the oddest times and seemed more afraid about a supposed 'curse' than anyone. Maybe so that she could get you to believe it, too. If I still had my proof, I could show you," Rachelle said, sending Harvey a significant look.

Harvey shook his head. "It wasn't enough, and it wasn't legal. But let's look at things another way. What if Rebecca and the show aren't the true targets?"

"What do you mean?"

"What if she wanted the show to be canceled for another reason?" Aaron said, understanding what Harvey was thinking.

"What reason?" Rebecca asked.

"Revenge," H.C. said. "Having to cancel would

hurt our image more than it would the Cromwell Collection."

"Kelli loves the fashion world. She used to have a sister who loved it even more," Rebecca said.

"What do you mean used to?" Aaron asked.

"She doesn't talk about her much, but I know she passed away when Kelli was young."

"I looked her up and didn't find any family tragedies," Rachelle said.

"Is Kelli Davis her real name?" Aaron asked.

"I used a hiring agency when I signed her," Rebecca said. "I assumed they did a background check."

"We'll have to do our own."

Rebecca shook her head. "I appreciate all this. I really do, but I still think Kelli isn't the one. She can be difficult sometimes, but she seemed genuinely worried about me and the show. Plus, while she's been here, all she's done is drink and flirt, right, H.C.?"

"Yes."

Candace laughed. "If she were a decade younger, she'd probably be on that party boat Aaron couldn't stand."

Aaron swore.

Everyone looked at him. "What?" Rebecca asked.

Candace's eyes widened. "But that was years ago. You don't think—"

Aaron nodded, his tone grave. "I do."

"What is it?" Rebecca asked.

"We think we know Kelli's motive."

Before Rebecca could ask what it was, Brandon burst into the room, his eyes swimming with tears. "He's dying! He's dying!"

The five adults stood and stared at him.

"Who?" Aaron demanded.

"Trident," he said. "You have to come quick."

Chapter 15

They all followed Brandon to the enclosure, where the iguana sat motionless. Aaron pulled out his phone and called the vet, who instructed Aaron to keep Trident moist and bring him over right away. Rebecca looked at Aaron, surprised that he had such direct access. He just said, "I have special privileges," then wrapped Trident in a soaked towel and put him in his traveling case. He gave him to Brandon to hold before the three of them piled in his car.

The veterinary hospital was located on the eastern side of St. James, and Aaron knew he needed to get there fast. "Hold on, everyone, I may have to break some traffic laws," he said, and just as he had done years ago, Rebecca found herself traveling the winding back roads of St. James.

After what seemed like hours, they pulled up in

front of the hospital and raced inside. The vet, Dr. Blaine Gladwell, a studious-looking man with long dreadlocks and round black glasses, stood waiting for them. Rebecca soothed Brandon while they looked on anxiously as Dr. Gladwell checked Trident.

After a quick examination, Dr. Gladwell shook his head and sighed. "I'll need to run some tests, but if my guess is correct, he's been poisoned."

"Poisoned?" Aaron asked, stunned. "How?"

"There are many ways for reptiles to be poisoned. Most of them are not deliberate. It could be the wrong food he was given, or his water."

"We haven't changed anything," Aaron said, looking at Brandon.

"I haven't done anything differently." A tear threatened to roll down his cheek.

"Have you changed his environment?" Dr. Gladwell asked.

"No," Aaron said.

"Is he going to die?" Brandon asked, no longer able to hold back the tears.

"I don't know," Dr. Gladwell said. "Since I don't know what made him sick yet, we'll give him some intravenous fluids to keep him hydrated, and something to help his body absorb whatever it is he may have eaten. We'll need to keep him here. With his age and how poorly he's looking, things could go either way. I'll have someone watch him overnight. There's not much more we can do but wait."

Back home, after tucking Brandon in bed, Aaron couldn't help wondering why what was happening to Trident didn't sit well with him. "First he goes missing, and then he gets sick. It doesn't make any sense."

"The statue," Rebecca said, meeting him in the hallway.

"What?"

"That's something new in Trident's cage," she said, heading there. "Your sister was showing me something she'd been given by one of the models who got sick when she went to the States. She thought it was ugly and planned to throw it away, but instead she put it in Trident's cage as part of the decoration."

They both went out back and entered Trident's cage. There, Rebecca noticed the statue had fallen into Trident's water dish, and a small piece of one of the ears had broken off.

Aaron snatched it up and swore, angered that something seemingly so harmless could do such damage.

"It may not be the reason."

"We'll have to find out," Aaron said, returning inside. He grabbed his jacket. "I'll drive it over to the hospital and leave it for Dr. Gladwell. He can check it out and see if it could be the cause. I hate leaving you here alone."

"I'm hardly alone. There's your grandmother and Brandon and—"

"I mean without me."

"I'll be fine. I can look after myself, and I can look after them, too, if necessary."

"Thanks," he said, reassured. Then he gave her a quick kiss before he left.

Once Aaron was gone, Rebecca went upstairs to check on Brandon. When she entered his bedroom, she saw that his bed was empty. She looked around, but couldn't find him.

"Brandon, where are you?" she called out softly.

She didn't want to wake Aaron's grandmother, whose bedroom was only two doors away. There was no response. Rebecca began to panic, then she noticed his blanket was missing but his slippers were still in his room. She hurried downstairs and checked the hallway closet. His jacket was gone. She quickly put on her coat and grabbed a flashlight from the top shelf in the closet and headed out back. As she approached Trident's cage, she heard the soft sounds of Brandon crying.

"Brandon, you are a crafty one," Rebecca said. "Your father and I were just here and didn't see you."

"I hid."

"Why? What are you doing in here?" she asked, opening the cage door to let herself inside. He was huddled under his blanket in the far corner of the shed, where the temperature was still warm.

"He's going to die. I know it."

"We don't know that, Brandon. The doctor said we will have to wait and see."

"But I didn't do anything wrong."

"Nobody said you did."

"Then why did he get sick?" He sniffed.

"I don't know. Sometimes things just happen."

"I don't want him to die."

"I know. Why don't we go back into the house and…"

Brandon shook his head and held his blanket tighter. "No, I want to stay here until Trident returns."

Rebecca sensed that arguing wouldn't work and decided to just go along with the situation. She held him close and let him rest his head on her lap.

After only a couple of minutes, he was sleeping

soundly. She carefully wrapped him up in the blanket, gently carried him into the house and put him in his bed.

"Thanks for looking after Brandon for me," Aaron said when he returned and Rebecca told him about Brandon's mini-adventure. They sat in the living room, neither of them ready to go to bed yet.

"You don't have to thank me again," Rebecca said, affectionately stroking his leg. "I know he's an important part of your life."

Aaron covered her hand. "So you're saying you have no choice?"

"No, I'm saying it's an honor that you trust me with your son."

Aaron closed his hand over hers. "He likes you."

"And the feeling is mutual." She sighed and looked at the blank TV screen.

"What is it?"

Rebecca hesitated, then said, "I hate to bring this up, but is there something you're hiding from me?"

Aaron looked at her, suddenly wary. "What do you mean by that?"

"I still don't believe Kelli is the one we should be looking at regarding the sabotage," Rebecca said.

Aaron released her hand and folded his arms. "That's because you've never been betrayed by someone you trust."

"But why don't you trust my judgment?"

"Because I prefer to trust the facts."

"What are the facts, really?"

"She's got the means, she was around and available and your sister found those incriminating items."

"You still haven't told me the motive."

"Until I get to confer with my investigator, it's still just speculation, but—"

"Say it straight. What do you and Candace know?"

"Kelli could be on the island to avenge what happened to her sister. There was a case about an assault that happened on the party boat ten years ago. The police's handling of the incident didn't go well."

"It was covered up?"

"Not by us, but…it wasn't pretty. Things like assaults against visitors are bad for St. James, and they tend to disappear from the headlines, if they even make it there. By tomorrow I should know Kelli's real name."

"But I'm telling you, in my gut, I don't think Kelli would do this to me."

Aaron's cell phone buzzed. He glanced down and read the text, then replied and put his phone away. "We just got our motive. That was my investigator. Kelli's last name isn't Davis, and she's related to an old case."

"That's still not proof—"

Aaron stood, agitated. "It's motive and that's all we need to get an arrest."

Rebecca stared up at him, horrified. "You're going to have her arrested?"

"Of course. What else do you expect me to do? Invite her over for tea and have her explain things?"

"At least let me talk to her."

"No, you stay away from her and let me deal with this. You may not like the way I do things, but I know how to take care of my family, and I know how to take care of you."

"By destroying someone close to me because you're so determined to have a suspect?"

"I'm not trying to destroy anyone. I'm only trying to get answers, and that's the end of it," he said, then stormed out of the room.

He couldn't understand why Rebecca wouldn't trust him, wouldn't listen to him. He started up the stairs, knowing that for the first time in days he'd be sleeping alone. But he halted when he saw his grandmother sitting on the stairs.

"What are you doing up?"

"I couldn't help overhearing."

"Trident's at the vet," he said, guessing she'd wonder about the commotion over the iguana. "We won't know anything until morning. Go back to sleep."

"That's not what I was talking about," she said, standing. "I heard you and Rebecca."

"It's nothing. Just a simple disagreement."

"But it bothers you, doesn't it?"

Aaron felt his temper flare, remembering Rebecca's accusations against him. "She's not being rational. She doesn't understand how important this is to me."

His grandmother gently touched his shoulder and said, "You were this way with Ina, too."

Aaron took a deep, steadying breath. "Careful, Nan. I'm not in the mood for this."

"Sometimes you need to listen rather than just talk," she continued, unafraid of his dark mood. "Evidence isn't always what you see it to be. I sense that you need her. Don't let this push her away from you."

"My job is to protect her, no matter what she thinks of me. Even if I have to push her away to be able to.

Night, Nan," he said, softening his words with a kiss
on her cheek before walking up the stairs.

He knew that what happened with Ina was different. She didn't want to listen to him, and what she saw
as him holding on tight was his way of being there
for her. He hadn't meant to suffocate her. But if Rebecca was feeling the same way, then his decision to
remain single was the best for him.

Stubborn, stubborn, stubborn. How could he be so
stubborn? He was wonderful in so many other ways,
but this trait was infuriating. Rebecca stood staring
out the window, unable to go to the room she'd been
sharing with him, even though she knew he probably
wouldn't be there. She needed to sleep, but couldn't.
This moment was so unlike ten years ago when she'd
hoped the night would never end. Now the night
seemed to last forever. She heard the soft sound of
footsteps and turned to see his grandmother.

"Did you want to watch TV?" Rebecca asked.

"No, I wanted to see you and talk to you about
Aaron."

"There's really nothing you need to say. I know
he's a good man and—"

"I didn't come here to defend his character. I don't
believe I need to. I just want you to understand a few
things."

Rebecca sat down and folded her arms. "So that I
won't feel like strangling him?"

She smiled. "Yes. Has he told you much about his
ex-wife, Ina?"

"No."

"She was a shock to all of us. She was completely

different from Aaron. Ina was wild and reckless, which at first thrilled him and then became the main contention in their marriage. She would go out all night and meet strangers, and she used her looks as a model to get whatever she wanted. She loved traveling the world. Aaron was always nervous, because he knew of the dangers out there, but he couldn't get her to settle down, even when she became a mother. That was the beginning of the end for them. She'd enjoyed the first month of motherhood until the joys of it were swallowed by the realities of not being the center of attention.

"When Brandon was two months old, she was back on the party scene and nearly lost her life twice—once in a drunk driving accident, and the second time after using a dangerous mixture of drugs. When Aaron put his foot down, alienating her suppliers and the shady friends she was hanging out with, she filed for divorce. She gave up custody of Brandon, and she told Aaron that she didn't want to be burdened with a child. She said she was too young, that she had too much living to do to just become someone's mother."

"But I'm nothing like Ina," Rebecca said.

"No, but Kelli is, from what I've overheard and seen. He sees her as dangerous to you. So don't be too harsh with him. All the Wethers men have been trained to do the same—honor and protect. They are bound by the courage and spirit of those who have gone before them. I'm sure you've heard about the great pirate Pierre LaCroix. Well, he was one of our great ancestors, as was Maureux. Our capital is named after him. They were men who fought for the very existence of St. James. They and others like them shed their blood fighting to protect what was theirs. That same blood runs in Aaron's veins. You can question his methods, but never question his devotion to you."

A light tapping on the door woke Rebecca from a restless sleep. She glanced at the clock, surprised by how early it was. "Come in," she said in a groggy voice, then sat up in surprise when Aaron came in.

"I just heard from Dr. Gladwell," he said.

She swallowed and waited, unable to read in his expression whether the news was good or bad. "And?"

"It's good news," he said with a soft smile. "Trident is beginning to respond to treatment, and the statue was the source of the poisoning. When it had fallen over into the drinking water, some of the phosphorus material seeped into the water and was slowly getting into Trident's system, killing him. They will keep him in the hospital a few more days, then Brandon can go get him and take him home. He's not awake yet. I thought I'd let you tell him at breakfast. They're sending the statue back to us in case we want it."

"Where are you going?" she asked, now noticing that he was wearing his jacket, but the moment she asked the question she knew the answer and regretted it. Seeing him getting ready to leave caused her to feel an odd loss. She'd grown used to having him constantly by her side. "Never mind."

"I have someone who will take you to the exhibit hall and be with you until I'm free."

She wanted to beg him to change his mind, but

knew he wouldn't. "Okay," she said, hating the distance that had come between them. But she didn't know how to close it.

Chapter 16

Kelli was enjoying an early-morning swim when a shadow blocked her sunlight. She glanced up and saw Aaron.

"Changed your mind? Care to join me?" she asked with a flirtatious grin.

"The snake was a mistake."

"What?" she asked, getting out of the water. She grabbed a large towel and wrapped it around herself before sitting down.

"I can explain away the stage malfunction, but the snake was a mistake. That is considered attempted murder."

"What? I don't understand."

"That's what you can be charged with."

"I don't know what you're talking about. I would never hurt Rebecca."

"But you wanted to hurt me?"

"No."

"I'm sorry about your sister."

Kelli paused, as if he'd struck her. "How did you…? You have no right to talk about her."

"The party boat had nothing to do with Red Beacon Hotel."

"I never said it did."

"You wanted to get back at us," Aaron continued, "because you think we covered up what happened to your sister, and you were angry."

"Yes, I was. My sister left St. James broken. Coming here was supposed to be one of the best times of her life, and instead she was assaulted. She never recovered, and she killed herself two months later. I almost couldn't believe it when Rebecca decided to set her show here. Suddenly all the memories came flooding back, and I wasn't sure I could handle it. But I wanted to prove that I could face the past—especially you. I found your name in her diary, along with Red Beacon Hotel. Back then, it wasn't a grand resort like it is now."

Aaron froze, amazed that her sister had written his name down. He still remembered everything—that night on the boat, a young coed who was a little tipsy but having fun. "I'm a woman now. I can do whatever I want," she'd told him.

"But you still have to be careful."

"You're one of the babysitters, right?"

"A chaperone."

"A pretty name for the same job. But you're to look after us."

"I do my best." He took her drink. "No more of

these, and careful of those guys," he said, then glanced up and saw Rebecca go overboard. "Excuse me," he said before racing off and getting caught up in her rescue. He'd completely forgotten about the other young woman.

Kelli watched his face, amazed. "You remember her?"

"Yes," he said with a heavy sigh of regret. "I never forgot her."

"You were there to protect her. And you failed. You left her all alone."

"I didn't mean—"

"It doesn't matter. When I think of her all alone after being raped and beaten, with no one to take care of her, it makes me so angry. Did you think she deserved it? Did you—"

"I didn't know, honest. There were so many people on the boat, and I was nervous about how it was being operated, but it didn't belong to us. It was owned and operated by another company. Thankfully, after several other charges of assaults on visitors, the company went out of business. That night, once I saw Rebecca go overboard—"

"Rebecca? Rebecca was there?"

"She was trying to escape the same fate as your sister, but she decided to be more daring."

"So you didn't just leave my sister alone?" Kelli asked.

"No. I wouldn't have done that."

Kelli covered her face in her hands. "I wish that made me feel better. When will the pain go away?"

"Why did you wait so long for your revenge? I

know you've come to the island many times before. You could have done something then."

Kelli looked at him, confused, her eyes red rimmed. "Revenge? I come to the island every year on the an- niversary of my sister's death just to remember, and do the things she can't. It took me two years before I could come to St. James, and it was only this year that I had the courage to visit the Red Beacon."

"You tried to sabotage the show to get back at me."

Kelli shook her head. "No, I didn't."

Aaron's voice hardened. "Kelli, no more lies."

"I'm not lying. I'd never hurt Rebecca."

"You were seen going into town to see Mama Soo." Mama Soo was known for making native potions, and it was her house that H.C. had seen Rachelle leaving.

"For good luck. She gave me a lizard, but it es- caped."

"A lizard...not a snake?"

"No. And I bought a piece of jewelry that was sup- posed to help me get rid of bad spirits. I swear I had nothing to do with the sabotage. Mama Soo warned me about the Wetherses, and I thought Rebecca might get hurt like my sister did, that's all. Please believe me."

Aaron hesitated as pieces started to come together. Kelli going into town would look suspicious to any- one, especially Rebecca's sister. She probably asked Mama Soo why Kelli visited her, but he knew that Mama Soo would never reveal what went on between her and her clients. "Did you call the TV station?"

"Why would I do that?"

Aaron swore. He believed her, but he didn't want to. He hated the thought that the person who was behind all this was still at large. He hated not knowing who it was, or why they'd done all this. He couldn't let his guard down, not until the show was over and Rebecca was off the island.

"Where's Rebecca?" Kelli asked, studying his face.

"At the exhibit hall. Don't worry, I have someone watching her, and security is tight."

"So far it's worked. Nothing has happened."

"And I intend to make sure it stays that way," Aaron said, his words a promise.

Harvey had just finished the final run-through as the announcer when he saw a message from Rachelle asking him to meet her. He excused himself and found her by the cove.

"I guess I should be going," she said, "but I wanted to see you first."

"So soon?" he asked, hating the thought of her leaving. "Why would you leave before your sister's show?"

"I never stay for her shows. I don't want anyone spotting me."

"You could wear a disguise," he said with a smile.

"I also have to get back to my grandmother."

"Oh."

"But are you free for lunch?"

"Yes."

A half hour later, the two met in town at Bawley's Jerk Favorites, the same location where they had eaten the jerk chicken legs.

"H.C., you want my special?" Edmund asked, greeting them with a knowing smile.

"Yes."

"What's the special?" Rachelle asked.

"Baked fish and breadfruit, wrapped in banana leaf."

"Sounds delicious." And it was. Edmund, sensing romance in the air, added his own flair with two glasses of homemade ginger ale and fresh sliced pineapples with mango-flavored ice cream for dessert.

"We're not all sun and sand and resorts here," Harvey said, looking out at the blue waters. He saw a man walking his goat and an escaped rooster pecking its way along the beach. "We have a thriving community of excellent schools, hospitals and stores."

Rachelle grinned. "Are you trying to sell me on the island?"

"Yes," he said, his tone and gaze without humor. "I have an aunt who works as a nurse at one of the finest nursing facilities here, if you were ever interested in moving."

"And why would I do that?"

He shrugged. "Maybe if you met someone you wanted to be with."

She playfully nudged him. "But why would I move? Why wouldn't *he* move?"

"Because he makes a lot of money and would be able to provide a good living for you and your family. You're a freelance graphic designer, so you can live anywhere."

She chewed on a piece of the breadfruit for a moment, considering it, then said, "It's a risk. He could grow tired of me."

He shook his head. "That won't happen."

"You sound like a romantic."

He rested a hand over his heart. "The moment I

saw you, I knew you were the only woman for me. I know I'm a lot older than you, but I'll be good to you, I promise you that."

She playfully nudged him again. "Your age doesn't bother me."

"It may bother others."

"I don't care. I like my men seasoned."

He flashed a shy smile. "I'm glad."

"But I still have to think about it."

"Don't think too long," he said.

"Because you'll change your mind?"

"No, because otherwise I have to start looking for another job in the States."

She laughed until she realized he was serious. "Oh, H.C.," she said, looping her arm through his and resting her head on his shoulder. "I don't know what to say."

"Say you feel the same. Even if it's a lie."

"I would never lie to you." She lifted her head and looked at him. "And I do feel the same. I guess it can't be helped." She covered her face and groaned. "I shouldn't do this. You'll make me miss my flight."

"You can always catch another one."

She let her hands fall and looked at him. "What's her name?" Rachelle asked.

"Who?"

"Your aunt. Before I go, I want to see this facility you're talking about. They may not have space."

H.C. jumped to his feet as if on springs. "I'll make sure they do. I should also show you where I live. We can get home care if you want. After the wedding, we can decide on which district you'd like to settle in permanently. I've lived as a bachelor, so we may need to find a more family-friendly place."

Rachelle stared at him with a look of both joy and confusion. "H.C., you don't know what you're taking on."

"Yes, I do. Most of my life has been about work, and now I'm making room for love."

Aaron found Rebecca exactly where he expected to—talking to the caterers. She'd been against the idea of him going to see Kelli, and he'd expected to have her in handcuffs instead of letting her go. He knew that would make Rebecca happy, since she'd been frosty since their fight. When she saw him, she said something to the chef, then walked over to him.

"Did you do it?" she asked. "Did you go and see Kelli and arrest her?"

"Yes and no."

"You must feel proud of yourself—wait, what?"

Aaron nodded, resting his hands on his hips. "I did go and see her, but no, I didn't have her arrested. I was very proud of myself until I discovered you were right."

"What?"

"After talking to her, I don't think she did it, either."

"You didn't have her arrested?"

"Isn't that what I just said?"

"I want to hear it again."

"Couldn't you just say 'I told you so'?"

Rebecca shook her head with a smile tugging on her mouth. "No, this is better. You didn't have her arrested, right?" she asked one more time, just to be sure.

"No, I had police standing by, but I wanted to talk to her first."

"Must be nice to have that kind of power."

"It is, when it works."

Rebecca snapped her fingers, satisfied. "I knew you had your doubts."

"How?"

"Because you still had someone watch me. If Kelli had been behind all that has been going on, you wouldn't have."

Aaron rubbed the back of his neck. "That doesn't make me feel better."

"Nothing has happened. Maybe the person has left the island."

"I don't like unanswered questions."

She wrapped her arms around his neck, her mouth spreading into a smile. "At least now we can kiss and make up."

He removed her arms. "Not yet. I'm on duty."

Rebecca was about to try to persuade him to go off duty when her cell phone rang. She answered it. "Hello, Rachelle."

"I'm getting married and moving to St. James."

Rebecca held her cell phone to her ear, not sure she'd heard her sister correctly. "Wait, did you just say that you're thinking of coming back and living here?"

"Yes. Oh, Rebecca, H.C. is the most wonderful man. I know I'll be happy with him, and we've talked about Gran and I know this environment will be good for her. I can work anywhere, so it won't be any trouble. I know he's not dashing and gorgeous, but he's so sweet, and his brown eyes make my heart melt."

"I'm happy for you," Rebecca said, acutely aware that Aaron could hear what her sister was saying.

"And if it works out with Aaron—"

"Aaron isn't as impulsive as H.C.," Rebecca said, sending Aaron a tremulous smile, embarrassed. "He had one bad experience with marriage."

"You could convince him to marry again."

"I really have to go. We can talk later."

Her sister swore. "He's there, isn't he?"

"Uh-huh."

"Good. He's crazy about you. It's obvious," she said, then hung up.

"Your sister?" Aaron asked.

"Yes," Rebecca said, putting her phone away. She didn't want to discuss what she had just heard. She had to focus on the show; the catering was set and the runners knew what to do. Now she just needed to see the set. After the accident, she'd let Aaron work with the set designer while she dealt with publicity and other tasks. But the moment she saw what he had done, she hated it.

Rebecca looked at the stage, horrified. It was all wrong.

"I'm going to kill him," Rebecca mumbled, turning to find out where Aaron was, but he'd strangely disappeared. She couldn't see him, but knew he was there. He probably knew how she'd react. She'd have to call him. She took out her cell phone.

"Put that away," Melanie said. Rebecca turned to her stage manager.

"Why? It's—"

"What he's done is amazing. I saw a tiny fragment of what he has in mind when he was practicing with the technical team, and I am getting the girls ready now."

Rebecca motioned to the stage. "He's going to ruin my show."

"No, this is brilliant."

Rebecca waved her hand in front of her, stunned. It wasn't like Melanie to give someone praise. "How can this be brilliant? It's just a stage. A plain, boring stage."

"Exactly. It will make your clothes look even more spectacular. I know that you're known for your gallery showings, but this will be something new for people to see. Don't you think your clothes should speak for themselves?"

"But everyone else has the same black background and—"

"Yes, sometimes there's a reason for tradition. The girls are already taking to it." She gestured to a volunteer, and moments later the models began walking onto the stage.

Melanie frowned. "My God, who taught you how to walk? A damn mummy?" She pointed to another. "And you, learn some rhythm. Count in your head if you have to. I need to see you float." She turned to Rebecca. "They'll be much better in two days."

"Stop being so harsh. They're doing their best, and you're right, the clothes look great."

"They'd look even better if you'd had the other three models. But leave this in my hands, and this collection will be all over the web. That's what I do." She turned to the group. "Faster. Why is the change taking so long?"

"Sorry, ma'am."

Melanie rolled her eyes. "Amateurs. Look at her," she said, pointing to a woman helping a model change. "She can hardly dress herself. How can she expect to dress others?"

"You don't have to push them so hard."

"I want excellence. And the only way I get it is when I demand it. You know, I have connections. I can get you a better assistant," she said, glancing at Kelli, who was helping one of the runners with their headset.

Rebecca felt relieved that Kelli still wanted to work even after such a painful conversation with Aaron. She remembered holding her and crying a little as she told her more about her sister and what St. James had meant to her. She now saw her in a new light, not just as a flighty, flirtatious woman but someone who wanted to live life fully for both her sister and now for herself. Melanie didn't know about the suspicions that had been cast on Kelli. Her feelings were personal.

"I don't know why you never liked her," Rebecca said.

Melanie sniffed. "She's not hungry enough. I could get you a girl willing to lick your boots if you asked her. That's dedication."

"No, that's scary."

Melanie gestured toward Kelli. "She doesn't have fashion in her blood. She doesn't eat, drink and live it."

"I don't want someone who wants to be a designer. Besides, she's efficient and good at what she does."

"From the looks of her, she doesn't want to be anything but one man's wife and another man's mistress. Unfortunately, she has all the equipment to pull it off."

"Retract the claws. I'm not getting rid of her."

"You have more courage than I do. I wouldn't want a woman like that around my man."

Rebecca frowned. "You've lost me. My man?"

Melanie shrugged. "I heard that you're living with the owner."

"The owner of what?" Rebecca asked, feigning innocence.

Melanie made a dramatic gesture around the hall. "Of the resort. Adam—"

"Aaron," Rebecca corrected. "And I'm hardly living with him," Rebecca said, keeping her voice low. "He just let me stay in his house because of what has been happening."

"I also heard Aaron killed the snake with a knife."

Rebecca made a *tsk*ing sound with her tongue. "You shouldn't believe everything you hear. They were scissors."

"And you fell into his arms, and he carried you out of the hall."

"Not exactly."

Melanie couldn't help a laugh. "I know. I made that part up. But it's being whispered that he's taken a keen interest in you."

"He was just being cautious."

"He may be," Melanie said slowly, "but are you?"

"What do you mean?"

"Do you know one of the reasons why you've risen so fast? It's not just because you're talented, but because your clothes tell a story. They invite people in. They're engaging. Just like you. You were raised by a grandmother who loved you, a sister who adored you. And you approach the world with an open heart. You

give everyone a chance, and that can be dangerous.
You have to learn to guard your heart. There are some
bad people in the world. You don't have to be frightened of them, but you do have to know they're there,
and they can really hurt you. Are you sure there's no
one with a grudge or something?"

"Positive."

"Fine, then be extra careful. Aaron is brilliant, and
he's rich. A man like that has enemies somewhere."

Later that afternoon, Rebecca met Rachelle at the
hotel where she'd been staying, and the two women
sat in the lobby. Aaron watched from a distance, giving them privacy.

"Why are you being so impulsive all of a sudden?"
Rebecca asked her sister.

"What do you mean?"

"Don't play dumb. I couldn't believe what I heard
over the phone. Are you really thinking of moving
to St. James on a whim, after meeting some man you
really don't know?"

Rachelle pursed her lips, angered. "Watch your
tone. H.C. is not just *some man*. It's not like he's someone I picked up off the street."

"I'm sorry, I didn't mean it like that," Rebecca said
quickly, not wanting to offend her sister.

"Don't you think Aaron's a good reference for
H.C.'s character?"

"Yes, but I'm concerned about you bringing Gran
to live here. The only place she's ever known is back
home in Delaware."

"Yes, but with her dementia, and all her friends

dead, the only people she knows are you and me and her brother, who visits her every now and then."

"I still think you're being too impulsive. At least think about it for a while before making things final."

"Too late. I've already accepted H.C.'s proposal and made arrangements to put Gran on the waiting list for one of the best nursing facilities here on St. James."

"I'm still not sure about this. I think—"

"Some of us don't need to be with someone forever before they know it's true love."

"True love?" Rebecca scoffed. "What do you know about true love?"

Rachelle tilted her head, studying her sister. "If I didn't know you better, I would think you were envious of me."

"No, it's not that. It's just that…"

"I know you love Aaron, and after seeing you with him, I think you've loved him for a long time. When are you going to tell me what happened on this island? Don't you think it's time we stopped having secrets between us?"

"You're right," Rebecca said with a sigh. "I am envious. I am envious that you've found a man who's willing to say he loves you and wants to spend his life with you. I'm envious that you'll get to call this island home while I'll have to leave."

"You don't have to."

"I'm not going to cling on to Aaron like a piece of seaweed. And I'm not going to pretend that I wish he'd ask for me." She wiped away a tear and plastered on a smile. "But now that I've gotten that off my chest, I can admit that I'm happy for you." She hugged her sister.

Rachelle hugged her back. "Don't stop dreaming, little sister. Anything can happen."

Chapter 17

A sliver of the moon hung low in the sky as Candace, Aaron and Rebecca sat on the veranda.

"The show is tomorrow night," Candace said. "So far nothing has gone wrong."

"Nothing will go wrong," Aaron said, staring at the ugly statue that had arrived from Dr. Gladwell.

Candace laughed. "You should have seen H.C.'s face when he saw Kelli. He couldn't believe you didn't have her arrested."

"I explained it to him," Aaron said, turning the statue upside down.

"I still don't understand what changed your mind."

Aaron sent Rebecca a look. "Let's just say I had my doubts."

"Why do you keep staring at that thing? I feel so bad about how it made Trident sick."

"You wouldn't have known it could poison his bowl," Rebecca said.

"Where did you get it anyway?" Aaron asked.

"From one of the models. Sareta. Yes, that's right. Sareta Monay."

Aaron paused. "Who?"

Candace grimaced. "I knew I shouldn't have told you."

"You hired a Monay?"

"They're not all bad. And she seemed perfect."

"You know that the Monay clan is bad news."

"Why?" Rebecca asked.

"The Monays are a family of smugglers, although they have several legitimate businesses here on the island. Candace knows I never work with them because doing so always causes trouble."

"I'm sure it's just an ugly little statue."

"Let's see." He tapped the statue against the ground, cracking it open. He pulled out some cotton, and then the corner of his mouth quirked in a cynical grin.

"What?" Candace said.

He poured the contents into his palm—precious stones, just as he suspected.

"I think we've solved our problem," Candace said.

"Why did they come after me?" Rebecca asked, stunned.

"They always start subtle, then make their threats more pronounced," Candace said. "I guess they thought Aaron was keeping what belonged to them."

"I never thought I'd witness something like this in real life. This is just like in a story."

Aaron gripped the stones in his hand until his knuckles turned pale. "Yes, too much so. I feel like I read this in a book somewhere." He poured the gems back into the statue and stood with controlled fury. "Excuse us," he said to Rebecca, then yanked his sister up from her chair and pulled her into another room.

"What were you thinking?" he demanded. "Were you even thinking when you did this?" he asked, tapping the side of his forehead.

"Did what?"

He pointed at her. "Trident didn't fit. That was your first mistake."

"What?"

"I always wondered why Trident didn't fit. Now I know it's because of you. You always have to go over the top. I would never have guessed if you hadn't stolen a scene from one of the stories from our childhood."

Candace held up her hands as if to calm him. "Aaron, just listen."

"Was any of this real?"

She bit her lip. "Some of it."

"How much?"

"The announcer really did get drunk and get in a fight."

Aaron tightened his hands into fists. "Candace," he said in a low, ominous tone.

"Aaron, I—"

"Why did you do this?"

"I couldn't stand the thought of you marrying Martha, so I knew I had to do something."

"So you came up with this whole charade?"

"It worked, didn't it?"

He headed for the door. "Not after Rebecca finds out."

Candace grabbed his arm, stopping him. "She can never know about this."

"Why not?"

"Because I always felt it was my fault you two didn't end up together, so I wanted to find a way to make it right."

"By threatening her life? This time you've gone too far. The stage mishap—you could have killed someone. You nearly did. And the thing with the poisonous snake—"

"How was I supposed to know the guy I hired was color-blind? He got the wrong snake. Lucky he didn't kill himself." She rubbed her hands together nervously. "As for the stage thing, it was under control until Rebecca decided to barge onto the stage when she wasn't supposed to be there. Luckily, you were there to save her."

Aaron couldn't talk. He could barely look at her. At that moment, all he could think of was how scared Rebecca had been and how he'd felt her body tremble, as she tried to pretend that she wasn't frightened.

"Rebecca has a right to know about this. We nearly arrested her assistant, H.C. was put in jail, her sister was worried sick."

"And you got to spend time with her."

"And it was all based on a lie."

"But what you two feel is real."

Aaron folded his arms. "Rebecca deserves better than this."

"Why do you think I put Trident in her villa? You

were so determined to stay away from the show, and I had to find a way to get you to see her."

"So you turned me into her fake hero."

"No, you really did save her. I told you the snake—"

"Was still all smoke and mirrors. I knew I shouldn't have trusted you. You just like to cause trouble."

"Don't pretend that you didn't like some of it. You were in your element protecting her. I was only trying to help."

"You mean like the last time you tried to help me ten years ago? Didn't I warn you about playing with people's lives?"

"I was—"

"Stop thinking about yourself, and truly look at what you've done. You dug up Kelli's painful past and almost had me arrest her."

"I knew you'd find out the truth, and I'm sure she's glad she can now heal."

"And H.C. was jailed, and Rachelle—"

"And he are going to get married and start a new life together. That wouldn't have happened without me."

"So you're not sorry at all, are you? You have no regrets." Aaron threw his hands up in frustration, knowing he'd never be able to convince Candace that what she'd done was wrong. "I knew you two were up to something. Did Mum even really hurt herself in Switzerland?"

His sister's coy smile said it all. "Is it wrong to try to create the happy ending I think my little brother deserves?"

"I can't keep this from Rebecca."

"You have to."

"Why?"

"Because you might face losing her again, this time for good."

Aaron stared at his sister for a long moment, weighing his options. "What am I supposed to say to her now?"

"Tell her that she's safe, and that you know who the culprit is, and she has nothing to worry about anymore, then—"

"Then?" he pressed, when she suddenly stopped.

"Then you can put chocolates on her pillow and candles around the bathroom, and spend one more special night together."

Aaron folded his arms, irritated that he liked the idea of spending more time with Rebecca before she left. "I'll make you pay for this, but not tonight."

Chapter 18

The day of the show, Rebecca didn't stand still, energized by the hot night she had spent with Aaron. She was up early and had a full breakfast before heading off to the exhibit hall to meet with Melanie. She was happy, and she didn't have to worry about Aaron following her around now that the mystery was solved, but she missed his presence. After meeting with Melanie, she walked through every step of the show, checking all the outfits and making sure they were arranged in the proper order. She then met with several of the seamstresses on hand who were responsible for on-the-spot repairs, such as sewing on or replacing loose or missing buttons and zippers, and then met with several of the volunteers to make sure that all the props needed by the models were marked and in their proper location. Several heels needed to be repaired at the last minute, and a few large straw handbags had to be replaced, as they had mysteriously gone missing.

They were later found hidden in the trunk of one of the models, who wanted to take them home as holiday gifts. Then Rebecca met with the makeup artists and hairdressers to discuss any issues they had. Everything looked chaotic, with half-naked models running here and there, and floor staff darting to and fro, creating a cacophony of noise. But what may have looked like pandemonium to an outsider was what the fashion world was all about. There were only two minor disturbances. One happened when one of her models threw a small tantrum when she couldn't locate her favorite hairspray. Rebecca came to the rescue, offering use of her own private supply. The other involved two male models who got in an argument over who would wear a pair of fitted leather pants. Rebecca assigned another male model, and ended the spat. Last, Rebecca met with H.C. to go over the script for the event, and to make sure of his pacing.

"You don't need to have too much flair. The clothes will speak for themselves, but you will need to be aware of what's going on." She went over in detail how important it was for the announcer to keep an eye on the models, and the sequence of the show, just in case the wrong outfit turned up on stage and he needed to improvise. H.C. assured her he was ready, and let her know he and Rachelle had spent many hours going over the script. He said he felt as prepared as he could be. Rebecca walked the exhibit hall one last time and said a silent prayer that everything would go well.

She still didn't like the backdrop Aaron had designed as a replacement, but there had been no time to create a brand-new set of colorful designs in time for the show. She exited the hall and returned to the villa to get changed for the evening. After a hot shower, she spent time curling and styling her hair, which she decorated with a thin, colorful scarf. She then stepped into one of her hand-painted silk pantsuits that hugged and emphasized her figure. She didn't want to over-shadow her own show, but knew she wanted to capture the attention of one person.

The night of the show, Melanie's words proved prophetic. Rebecca saw Aaron's genius. He had turned her fashion show into an extravaganza larger than she could have ever dreamed. While Rebecca had found the surroundings to be stark in comparison to the elaborate and colorful set design she had initially created, she was blown away by what she saw. Aaron had hired a leading set designer to use an infusion of color using the latest technology to deliver a series of digitally manipulated images that interacted with the stage and models, and adapted based on the clothing being shown. Just like his dioramas, a series of electrifying scenes were skillfully created on stage, not upstaging the fashions being shown, but instead emphasizing the colors and ingenious designs.

At the end of the three-hour event, Rebecca was swarmed by photographers and reporters, but she wished to be with only one person.

A few yards away, Aaron watched her, knowing this meant the end.

"My little brother, the hero," Candace said, kissing her brother on the cheek at the end of the show.

Aaron playfully pushed her away. "Cut it out."

"I knew I could trust you." She looked at Rebecca talking to a news reporter. "You've taken her to a whole new level."

"I just didn't want to see her fail."

"You did more than that."

"Why didn't you tell me she was Becca from all those years ago?"

"I wanted you to find out for yourself. You know I like to keep up with all the current fashion trends. I made it a point to follow Rebecca's career and jumped at the opportunity to host her show here."

He nodded, annoyed. "Right, that was part of your little scheme."

"It wasn't a scheme," she said, lowering her voice. "It was a plan. I wanted you to see what an amazing woman she'd become, and not just see her as the nineteen-year-old whose feelings you hurt."

"Hmm."

"You didn't do all this just out of guilt, right?"

"What do you think?"

"I'm never quite sure with you. She's leaving tomorrow."

"I know."

"What are you going to do about it?"

"Nothing."

"You can't just let her leave after all that I've done."

"Why not? You and I both know she doesn't belong here." He shot her a glance. "And it would serve you right."

"H.C. is going to marry her sister."

"I'm not H.C."

"I didn't say you were, but—"

"But what? You think a couple of days would make me forget why Ina left me? Why my last several relationships have failed? I can't pretend that we don't live very different lives, that we're two very different people."

"You're not as different as you think. When are you going to realize that you married Ina on the rebound?"

"I know I made a mistake."

"That's not what I mean. When you met her in Paris, you thought you were getting a second chance with Rebecca. Ina was Rebecca's replacement."

"I didn't think of her that way."

"Your mind may not have, because you thought she was too young, but your heart did. I guarantee you, if you hadn't met Rebecca first, you would have seen how flashy and fake Ina was. Rebecca is the one for you. The fashion and the fame are all just trimmings. At the core, you're very much alike. Look at this. You're good, and you made her clothes look amazing. Not just any man could do that."

"I was glad to see her and help, but there's nothing more to it."

"You don't mean that. I know you want more."

"What I want and what I can get are two different things. Look at how beautiful and happy she is. She doesn't need me anymore."

"But look at all the trouble I went through to…"

"To what? Find me true love? Don't flatter yourself," he said, then left.

The balmy night air kissed her skin as Rebecca leaned against the balcony railing and listened to the sound of the ocean in the distance. Their last night together had been as sizzling as a summer storm, and she hated the thought of saying goodbye.

She felt his arms slide around her waist. "What are you doing out here?"

"Trying to will the night to never end."

"I know the feeling."

She turned and looked up at him. "But no matter how much I wish for that, I must face the dawn and accept the truth."

"The truth?"

"I've been waiting for you to ask me to stay."

"I'm not going to do that. I know your life isn't here. That would be selfish."

She kissed his chin and winked. "Selfish can be fun. You can start now."

"It's wrong."

"Why are you making that decision for me? Let me choose."

"You once compared yourself to a dragonfly, and you're right. You need to be free."

"With you I am free. I'm free to be myself. I love this island and you and Brandon. Why won't you—"

"Because the novelty will fade."

"What?"

"One day, the constant sunshine will wear on you. You'll miss the changing of the seasons. You'll miss the sound of rush-hour traffic and the crush of crowds, going to a Broadway show or gallery."

"So what?"

"And one day you'll look at me in the same way. The way you feel about me is because of what happened. Because I helped you during a dangerous time. But when the danger's gone and days blend into others, you'll realize I'm not a hero, just an ordinary business-man. And it will weigh on you. The monotony will drag you down."

"You poor thing. You don't understand me at all. I don't love you because you rescued me. I don't love you because you protected me or because you're rich. I love you because you make me feel like no one else. Because I like your company, and I did from that night ten years ago, and I can imagine growing old with you. What others might find boring, I find endear-ing. But I can't force you to ask me to stay if you don't want me to. Just remember this. I love you. Come to me when you're ready to believe that."

"I don't know how to thank you," Rebecca said to H.C. as the taxi driver closed the trunk to drive her to the airport.

"I just did my job," he said in a humble tone.

"You did more than that."

"I'm sorry Wethers couldn't be here."

"That's okay, we already said our goodbyes."

"Give him time. He'll come to his senses."

"Maybe."

"Don't forget about the festival," H.C. said sud-denly as she got settled in the backseat.

She looked up at him, startled. "What?"

"Our festival. If you ever want to come back and visit, it's worth seeing."

"I'd love to."

"There's more information on our website. You'd always have a place to stay. Just let me know."

She waved goodbye, then stared out the window, remembering the last time she'd left the island. She'd been near tears then, too. She'd be back to see her sister and grandmother, but never for him. That chapter of her life had ended. She closed her eyes against tears and listened to the sound of the radio, wanting it to crowd out her painful thoughts.

"Rebecca?"

She heard Aaron say her name, and she opened her eyes. She glanced at the stocky driver and shook her head. Aaron was nowhere around. Had she dreamed it?

"Rebecca. I hope you're listening to this."

She stared at the radio, her heart racing.

"I don't know why it's taken me so long to admit this, and I know I made an idiot of myself ten years ago over the radio, but I had to let you know. I want you to stay, and I love you. I love you so much. You asked me to come to you when I'm ready to believe that you love me, but that's not the answer. I married too quickly and was reckless. That's what I don't want to do again. I told you I hate to wait, but I'm willing to wait for you…if you'll do the same. I want you to leave. I want you to live your life for a year. If you're still interested, I'm not going anywhere. That's how I'll know that this isn't just a novelty, but something more."

Over the next several weeks, Aaron kept his distance from his sister because he was still angered by her deception. When they did meet each other, he tried to be cordial.

"I need to talk to you about our entry in the Feast of the Saints parade," Candace said, coming into his office and taking a seat.

"Do what we always do," he said, keeping his gaze on his laptop screen.

"H.C. and I were thinking of doing something a little different."

"Why?" He wasn't in the mood for anything out of the ordinary.

"We… I mean Rebecca's sister, Rachelle, has offered to help us come up with a new design."

"What's wrong with the old one? We always win." He hadn't heard Rebecca's name for a while.

"I know, but we just want to tr—"

"Fine, go ahead," he said. "But don't try to do anything too extravagant, and keep it within budget." Candace jumped out of her seat, ran around his desk and gave him a kiss on the cheek.

"Thank you. You won't be sorry."

As he watched her go, Aaron wasn't sure he had done the right thing, but saying yes was at least the beginning of him forgiving her for what she had done. Since Rebecca left, Aaron had punished Candace by reducing her salary by half and forcing her to work in the hospitality division, and she had been remorseful and had tried, on several occasions, to let him know how sorry she was for her deception and for putting other people's lives at risk.

Chapter 19

A firework lit the sky in a brilliant array of color. Costumed figures paraded the streets to the sound of drums and horns. Aaron looked on with amusement.

"I still can't believe you gave her a year. An entire year. Why did you have to make it so long?" Candace said, standing next to him. She was dressed as the Queen of Sheba, wearing an elaborate shimmering gold costume and expensive jewelry.

Aaron sighed and rolled his eyes. "So you've been saying for the past three months."

"Yes, and I bet it's felt like three years to you."

He didn't want to admit that he regretted his terms. He wanted to give Rebecca her freedom, but he missed her more each day. He remembered when Brandon's teacher called him for a conference.

"What's the problem?"

"No problem. I just wanted to know the secret."

"Secret?"

"Your son's grades have improved in a way I've never seen before, especially in math. He went from failing to passing with flying colors, and he's even helping the other students."

"I see."

"He can't stop talking about Miss Rebecca. I wish I'd had the chance to meet her."

He'd left the school with a reluctant grin, remembering Rebecca telling him she was helping Brandon with his 'surprise.' It certainly was. He had known about Brandon's struggle with math, but didn't want to embarrass him, and wanted him to ask for help if and when he needed it. He'd had to stop himself from calling her.

"She's perfect for you," Candace went on with a sigh. "Rebec—"

Aaron nudged her, sending a glance to his son, who watched the crowd in delight. He wore a pirate's outfit, complete with a black eye patch and a bag filled with fake money and jewels. "Quiet, it took me nearly a month to get him to forget about her."

"He hasn't forgotten her. He just doesn't tell you anymore. It's true," she added when he gave her a look. "He still tells me about what they did together. He even thinks she'll show up."

"When?"

"Tonight."

"Why would he think that?"

Candace shrugged. "I don't know, but that's what he told me."

"I'd wondered why he was especially eager this morning. You should have told me."

"Why?"

"So he won't be disappointed. And—" He stopped when he saw an extraordinary float that looked like an exact replica of one of his dioramas. It was of an island princess surrounded by nature. He heard his sister gasp beside him.

"Do you see it?"

He couldn't nod or even make a sound. He couldn't believe the sight before him.

"Dad! Dad! She came!" Brandon said, jumping up and down. "I knew she wouldn't miss the festival. And isn't she beautiful?"

"Yes, she is."

Aaron followed the float to the end of the parade route, then when it stopped, he jumped on board.

Rebecca stared at him, unsure. "Don't be angry. I couldn't wait a year."

His resulting kiss let her know that he couldn't wait, either. "There's something I have to tell you."

"No, you don't."

"Yes, it's important. I don't want any secrets or lies between us."

She covered his mouth. "If it's about your sister, I already know. She told me."

"Everything?" he asked, doubtful, knowing his sister couldn't be trusted. "Did she tell you about the Monay mob family and the jewels and how she—"

"She made up a story just to get us together. Yes, she did. She told me how furious you were that you were afraid you were no longer my hero."

Aaron squeezed his eyes shut. "She shouldn't have told you that. I—"

Rebecca cupped his face. "You will always be my hero, no matter what happens."

He rested his forehead against hers. "Thank you," he breathed, his voice barely a whisper.

She blinked. "For what?"

"For saving my life that night ten years ago. I wasn't going to kill myself, but I was living other people's lives and not my own. After meeting you, I decided to take more risks and not be ashamed of how I felt. And you came back and saved me again, this time from myself."

She shrugged. "Some heroes need a sidekick."

"I don't want a sidekick. I want a wife."

"You could find one on the island."

"I'd rather steal one from the States."

"Spoken like a true pirate."

He grinned. "Yes," he said, then his lips brushed hers with a tantalizing invitation for more.

Epilogue

Rebecca and Rachelle looked at each other in wonder as they each stood in their wedding gowns. Their wedding day had finally arrived. Six months earlier, they had made a vow to get married on the same day. It was the first and only time they had made such an arrangement. For identical twins, they were extremely independent, and though they kept in touch, they led totally separate and independent lives. But on this day, they wanted to celebrate their bond as sisters.

After agreeing to marry H.C., Rachelle had flown back to the States to put things in order and make arrangements for their grandmother to move into the nursing home on St. James that H.C. had arranged for. But that didn't go as smoothly as they had hoped. Gran fell and had to be hospitalized briefly. While in the hospital, she developed pneumonia and became gravely ill.

"I don't know what to do," Rachelle told Rebecca over the phone. "Her doctor doesn't think moving her is such a good idea."

"We can postpone things until she gets better," Rebecca said.

"That could be a while. Maybe you and Aaron—"

"We can wait," Rebecca said. "I'm not going to let you handle this on your own like I have in the past."

"What's wrong?" Aaron asked, coming into the room.

"We may have to postpone the wedding. Gran fell and… What are you doing?" she asked when he pulled out his phone.

"Scheduling a flight out of here. It's about time I get to meet her, don't you think?"

"Do you really want to do that?"

He winked at her. "I want to give her a reason to heal quickly."

To Rebecca's surprise, his plan worked. He and Brandon charmed her grandmother, and she made a miraculous recovery. She grew stronger every day, completed physical therapy and was up and walking much sooner than the doctors expected. She was even lucid enough to want to play a role in the wedding.

"Who do you plan to use to walk you both down the aisle?" Gran asked out of the blue. The three of them had just returned from trying on their wedding dresses. Both brides were excited, just like when they were kids going shopping for the first time, but they decided not to have identical dresses—a joint wedding was enough.

"Uncle Oscar can escort the two of us," Rachelle said. They didn't have a large family, and the only uncle they had was more than delighted to be asked to play such an important role. Kelli was Rebecca's maid of honor, and of course Candace was one of the bridesmaids. Rachelle's maid of honor and bridesmaids consisted of several of her longtime friends, and just as with their wedding dresses, their bridesmaids did not wear identical dresses or colors.

H.C. and Aaron took care of the logistics for the event, since it was held in St. James, and they didn't disappoint the guests who attended. They held the ceremony on the beach, where a large, elaborate tent stood tall, decorated with an assortment of the island's exotic flowers, their fragrance scenting the air.

After exchanging their vows, the wedding party retreated to a rented, outdoor pavilion, where the two couples and guests partied all night. Brandon, who was the ring bearer for both brides, couldn't contain his excitement and stayed up until early the next morning. He was found asleep under one of the tables, exhausted from all the activity, with a big smile on his face.

Rebecca stood near the edge of the cliff, staring at the water, remembering who'd she'd been ten years ago standing at this same spot, heartbroken. She held her arms out and turned her face to the sun, feeling its warm rays on her skin. Two weeks ago, she'd returned from her honeymoon with Aaron, not realizing how much St. James already felt like home. She closed her eyes, then let out a shriek when someone swept her off her feet.

She stared at her new husband, confused. "What are you doing?"

"Saving your life," he said with a roguish grin.

"I don't need you to do that anymore." She wrapped her arms around his neck, love shining in her eyes.

"What do you need me to do?" he asked, his gaze melting into hers.

She brushed her lips against his. "I need you to help me make a new one."

* * * * *

A world of secret
passion awaits…

HEAT WAVE *of* DESIRE

YAHRAH ST. JOHN

KIMANI™ ROMANCE

California Desert Dreams

HEAT WAVE *of* DESIRE

YAHRAH ST. JOHN

Kimberley Parker is transforming her family's property into California's most exclusive A-list retreat. But one of the hotel's enigmatic guests is arousing more than her curiosity. Heir to a powerful financial dynasty, Jaxon Dunham knows he can't hide out forever. But when Jaxon finds himself the focus of scandalous headlines, he's forced to either trust his heart or walk away from a promising love…

California Desert Dreams

HARLEQUIN®
™ www.Harlequin.com

Available June 2015!

KPYSJ4050615

His game…
her rules!

The LOVE GAME

Regina Hart

Tyler Anderson is poised to take over his family's company. But first he must team up with self-made marketing consultant Iris Beharie. Landing the Anderson Adventures account could save Iris's fledgling PR firm. And as Tyler sheds his introverted image in the bedroom, things heat up in the boardroom. Amid distrust and treachery, is Ty ready to gamble everything on a love that's as real as it gets?

THE ANDERSON FAMILY

Available June 2015!

REQUEST YOUR FREE BOOKS!

2 FREE NOVELS
PLUS 2 FREE GIFTS!

KIMANI™
ROMANCE

Love's ultimate destination!

The first two
stories in the
Love in the Limelight
series, where four
unstoppable women
find fame, fortune
and ultimately...
true love.

LOVE IN THE LIMELIGHT

New York Times
bestselling author

BRENDA
JACKSON
&
A.C. ARTHUR

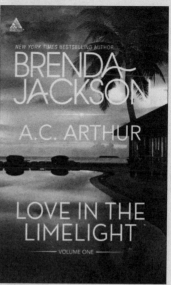

In *Star of His Heart,* Ethan Chambers is Hollywood's most eligible bachelor. But when he meets his costar Rachel Wellesley, he suddenly finds himself thinking twice about staying single.

In *Sing Your Pleasure,* Charlene Quinn has just landed a major contract with L.A.'s hottest record label, working with none other than Akil Hutton. Despite his gruff attitude, she finds herself powerfully attracted to the driven music producer.

Available now wherever books are sold!

www.Harlequin.com

KPLIM11631014R